MISHA

The City

KENT HAMILTON NUÑEZ

Ingrid,
  You are Awesome!!!
I'm so Glad I know you.
  Enjoy the read..

[signature]

iUniverse, Inc.
New York   Bloomington

Misha The City

Copyright © 2010 Kent Hamilton Nuñez

This is a work of fiction. All of the characters, names, incidents,
organizations, and dialogue in this novel are either the products
of the author's imagination or are used fictitiously.

iUniverse books may be ordered through booksellers or by contacting:

iUniverse
1663 Liberty Drive
Bloomington, IN 47403
www.iuniverse.com
1-800-Authors (1-800-288-4677)

ISBN: 978-1-4502-4853-2 (pbk)
ISBN:978-1-4502-4854-9 (ebk)

Printed in the United States of America

iUniverse rev. date: 8/12/2010

For my niece, Savannah Marie Torres A.K.A. Savy

Acknowledgments

With every great accomplishment my deepest motivation stems from the love of my family. As always my thanks to my mother, Maria and sisters, Shirley and Lisa, for their supportive love and Angela Gonzalez, a gem in my life.

I would also like to thank Lissette, Lee Chan, and Sara Evelyn for their input in my life for this book.

Additionally, this book could not have been written without the aid and inspiration of my brilliant muse and assistant, Megan Hanford.

Lastly, I thank Barbara Gottfried Hollander for her swift and generous editing contribution.

In loving memory of Luz Delgado

Prologue

On December 30, 1975, two anthropologists and their young Machiguenga Indian guide trekked along a narrow trail in the dense, sweltering Amazon jungle.

"Professor, we've been walking for hours. Do you have any idea where we're headed?" asked the teen-aged protégé, as he gasped for air. He adjusted the bulky duffle bag on his back.

"Nicolas, just keep up! I know we'll find it this time. I'm sure of it!" insisted the older man, who was in his late 50s. He wore a short, thick cotton jacket, beige trousers, a brimmed felt hat and round glasses.

For the last couple of months, both explorers had been searching for a long-lost pyramid mentioned in the lore of the Machiguenga natives of that region. The only problem was that the elder Indians—who were the guardians of that sacred place—did not allow any outsiders to see or even to know of the pyramid's location.

The young Indian guide slashed his way through the thick jungle with a sharp machete, and the two archeologists followed closely behind.

"Professor, you never told me how you managed to convince our guide to take us there," Nicolas said, looking behind him as the long jungle vines flung back and resealed the path in their wake.

"I promised him a fortune in gold," the older man replied.

"But Professor, we don't have any money, let alone gold!" Nicolas whispered.

"Let me worry about that," the professor replied. "Now, check your compass and tell me which way we're headed now."

Nicolas eyed the compass for a moment and answered, "West. We must be going further away from the Pini Pini River. I would say about four miles now."

"Jot it down," instructed the professor. "We'll need to know how to find this place again without him."

Suddenly, the Indian boy stopped slashing through the intertwined trees, looked back at Professor Garson, and pointed through the shrubbery.

The professor stepped forward and parted the large green leaves. "We've found it!" he whispered excitedly.

Just ahead of them was what appeared to be a large, steep hill, but was actually the sacred pyramid, almost entirely covered over by vegetation. Because the thick plant life had concealed the pyramid over the years, there was no way of seeing it from an airplane or from any helicopter searches.

"Nicolas, if the legends are true, this pyramid is older than the Great Pyramid of Egypt. Perhaps 12,000 years old."

"That's impossible," Nicolas retorted.

Professor Garson urged the Indian in his native language, "Take us inside."

The boy shook his head in response. With eyes wide with fear, he began to yell and exclaim in his native language. Obviously terrified, the Indian guide bolted back in the direction they had come from—superstition had overtaken his greed. "According to the Machiguengas, if anyone other than the highest priests enter the hidden pyramid, it will bring great misfortune upon them," mused the professor, quietly, almost to himself.

"Hey, come back here!" Nicolas yelled at the disappearing back of the guide. "Don't leave us here!"

"Let him go," Professor Garson said. "We don't need him anymore. And besides, now I don't have to pay him the gold that we don't even have." A sly grin slid across his face. Nicolas realized that this had been his plan all along.

He and Professor Garson made their way through the thick, lush groundcover and walked around the massive pyramid. On the right side of the pyramid, they found a small opening. Both pulled out their flashlights and braced themselves to climb into the pitch-black slit.

The entryway was only big enough for one to go through at a time, so Professor Garson gamely entered first and swatted away the thick cobwebs in the narrow passageway. Nicolas was close behind, and their flashlights slowly swept over a series of hieroglyphics on the surrounding walls. Nicolas noticed a large circular symbol with a stick figure of a man in the center of it, and a pyramid on top of him.

Seemingly uninterested in the hieroglyphics, the professor moved on down the passageway while Nicolas kept a close distance. Professor Garson clambered over dirt and rocks into a smaller chamber, where he saw crude drawings of skulls on the walls.

"Professor, how do you know where you're going?" Nicolas asked. "It's like you've been here before."

"We're here," said the professor, excitedly, without answering the question

"What are you talking about, Professor Garson? Aren't we here to study the entire pyramid?"

The professor placed his hands on the wall, feeling its grooves. "No... no, we came here to find something even more incredible. But first we must get behind this wall." He traced the spiral grooves with his fingers.

"But Professor, I don't understand!"

"Here it is!" the professor said as he pushed a loose stone through the wall.

The seemingly solid wall simply crumbled, exposing a hidden chamber.

"I knew it!" the older man exclaimed. He stepped inside the small room.

Off to the right of the space, barely lit by the two flashlights, was a rectangular tomb with a stone cover—about five feet long and three feet wide. The walls of the small room were riddled with drawings.

"Look at these." Nicolas eyed the pictographs closely. "They look like depictions of homes and buildings. And look over here." He pointed. "These could be agricultural diagrams for cultivating land. And the holes in this drawing appear to be star constellations. But wait a second!" He quieted to think for a moment. "It can't be!"

"What do you mean, Nicolas?" the professor asked as he searched for a weak spot on the stone cover of the tomb.

"You said this pyramid was older the Great Pyramids of Egypt. If that's true, then how could all of this knowledge be recorded on these walls?"

"What if I told you that these people were more advanced than the Roman Empire?" Professor Garson asked, smirking.

"That makes no sense. They would've left something behind, some kind of evidence of their sophistication," Nicolas replied.

"What if they couldn't? Now help me here," the professor requested, as he attempted to slide the stone cover of the tomb off to the side.

Nicolas put down his flashlight to help him in his effort. "Professor, what do you mean, they couldn't?"

"Harder, push harder!" the older man insisted.

"I *am* pushing. Just don't over-exert yourself," Nicolas urged.

The stone cover eased sideways slowly at first, then slid faster until it toppled over and shattered. Inside the stone cavity, they saw the mummified remains of a small human.

"What is this?" Nicolas asked, before noticing that the professor was sitting on the ground gripping his left arm. "Professor, are you okay?"

Sweating profusely, the professor clutched at his chest. "I— I think it's my heart."

"Your doctor told you that it was weak and that you shouldn't take this trip! But, you just *had* to come here!" Then, worried that he was stressing out the professor even more, Nicolas asked in a panic, "What should I do?"

"Go to the mummy and open its right hand," Professor Garson ordered, frowning. "I have to know if this is another one."

"Another one? What are you talking about?"

"Nicolas, please! Look in the mummy's right hand and tell me if there's anything in there." The professor was breathing laboriously.

"Okay, okay. I'll do it." Nicolas approached the coffin.

Standing on the right side of the tomb, Nicolas pushed away the thick cobwebs. Both of the mummy's hands were completely wrapped in cloth. Nicolas pulled off his backpack and fished around inside for his Swiss army knife. Reluctantly, he began cutting away at the bandages on the right hand.

"Professor, this is disgusting," Nicolas complained, while cutting through the ancient, blood-stained cloth.

"Is… there… anything… in his hand?" Professor Garson managed to ask between shallow breaths. He watched Nicolas struggle to rip off the thick, rotted swaddling. Then Nicolas yanked at something from inside the coffin. "Did you find it?" the professor asked desperately.

"I don't know what you were expecting me to find. There's just this black stone," Nicolas said, holding up a dark, dusty stone.

"Bring it here," Professor Garson croaked.

Nicolas handed him the stone and the professor winced as he polished it off with his shirt.

"*It is* another one!" the professor said with obvious delight, despite his discomfort.

"What is it?" Nicolas asked.

"Quick, look inside my private bag," the professor said.

"But you told me never to look inside that bag," Nicolas reminded him, nervously.

"Just do it," the professor snapped impatiently. His face had become deathly pale.

Nicolas unzipped the bag. Inside, he found a brown, leather-bound book and a small but heavy drawstring sack. "What is this?" he asked, holding up the sack.

"Look inside," the professor said, between groans.

Nicolas undid the strings and pulled out several jet-black, shiny stones. He turned his flashlight on them to inspect the stones closely. Symbols were carved on one side of each stone. Nicolas turned to the professor. "What are these?"

"Come here, flash your light onto this stone," the professor said.

The symbols on the stone they had just found were of the ancient Machiguengan language. The other stones were of a similar size and shape. He looked at the professor, confused. "Where did you find all these stones and what do these symbols mean?"

The professor grimaced and pressed his hand harder over of his heart. "Nicolas, listen and don't say a word—I don't think there's much time." He held up the newly found stone. "The symbols all mean the same thing—it's a name. This is the sixth stone I've found in my lifetime. I discovered the first when I was about your age. They were all hidden in pyramids around the world and they've always been entombed in the right hand of an enshrined human body."

"But professor, I don't—" Nicolas was interrupted by the older man.

"Listen, Nicolas! I found one in an Aztec pyramid, one in Pompeii…" He coughed roughly. "Even in pre-Inca civilization— Aaagh!" he yelled.

"Professor?" Nicolas whispered, worried.

Professor Garson whispered back, "And in a pyramid in Atlantis."

"What do mean? No one has ever found Atlantis," Nicolas told him.

"I did," the professor wheezed. "And do you know what all these civilizations had in common?"

"Well, it's been said they were all inexplicably destroyed… or simply disappeared," Nicolas said hesitantly.

"That's right, my boy, that's right," the professor told him. "And if you read my findings in the book you just took out of my bag, you'll discover that in every lost or destroyed civilization, there was a special person and a black stone.

"Okay, but what does it all mean?" Nicolas asked.

"After studying all of the pictographs and archeological evidence in each of the pyramids, I noticed they all implied roughly the same thing—that the person buried with the stone was somehow the destroyer of a particular civilization, the cause of its demise. The name on the stone is the name of the destroyer. All the stones were carved with the same name, only in different dialects. You can read it in my book. I've spent my entire life detailing everything about these individuals and the black stones—" The professor's eyes rolled back into his head and he began to convulse.

"Professor, professor!" Nicolas yelled as he shook his mentor. "Don't die! Please don't die!" He laid the professor flat on his back and attempted to perform CPR. "Can you at least tell me where Atlantis is or what I'm supposed to do with these stones?"

The professor said nothing, and exhaled his last breath.

Chapter 1

ON ROUTE 66, BETWEEN ST. Louis and Oklahoma City, a trucker was driving his semi-rig on a delivery to Los Angeles. The rain was pounding against the windshield. He glanced over at the digital clock near his rearview mirror, and then back out through his windshield. He had driven down that road many times before, but never in such bad weather.

"Two a.m. already?" he mumbled to himself.

The heavyset, bearded man pulled out his thermos while holding the steering wheel with his left hand, and poured coffee into a mug sitting in the cup holder. As he took a sip of coffee, he gazed at the passing white lines in the middle of the road. Then he spotted a drenched man wearing a hooded jacket standing on the side of the road just ahead. He turned on his high beams and slowed to a stop. It took the truck a minute to come to a complete halt on the slippery road. The driver opened the door and waved the hitchhiker inside.

The teenage boy entered the cab of the truck and sat in the passenger-side seat. "Thanks for picking me up." He brushed the water from his hair and glanced down at his soaked clothes. "Sorry for getting your seat wet," he told the driver.

"It's okay," the man said as he resumed driving. "This is the middle of nowhere. What are you doing out here, kid?"

"I was looking for a friend. My name is Tennessee, by the way."

"My name is Hamilton, but you can call me Ham," said the leather-faced trucker as he faced the road. "He must be a pretty special friend."

"Hamilton. Is that your first name or your last name?" asked Tennessee.

"It's my first name," the driver responded. "Long story short, my father wanted me to have his last name and my mom wanted me to have her last name. In the end, both my first and last names are my parents' last names," the trucker explained, and then asked, "Where you headed?"

"For now, I'm headed west," Tenny answered. Then he noticed the writing that filled the walls of the cab.

"You don't look like the typical wanderer," Ham told him.

"Why do you say that?" Tennessee asked, keeping his eyes on a poem written in black marker near the glove compartment.

"Most people hitching a ride look haggard, tired and lost. You don't look that way."

"Don't you think it's too soon to have an impression of someone?" Tenny asked.

"I have the gift of reading people quickly. I've always had a knack for it."

"So you pick up lots of hitchhikers?" Tenny asked.

"I make it my business to help people on the road," the trucker answered.

Tenny read the words on the wall just overhead: "*I see them as white papers walking. I wait to see the beautiful art they will become. The gray ones, those are the ones I offer a new canvas.*"

Tenny turned to Ham. "Did you write all this stuff?"

"When I get inspired, I write," Ham said, with a quick glance at his handiwork.

"What does this one mean?" Tenny asked, pointing at the words he'd just read.

"Well, it has to do with all the people I meet and my desire to help them." Ham took another sip of his coffee.

"What do you mean?"

"It's a bit hard to explain, but I've always felt compelled to help others. I see lots of lost souls on the road—drug addicts, prostitutes, runaways, and your occasional hard-core criminal."

"How do you help them?" Tenny asked.

Ham quickly eyed Tenny. "Okay, this is gonna sound crazy, but I instinctively know what they lack in their lives, and I become the mirror that shows them."

"Mirror?"

"I tell them what they need to hear in order to help them— that's if they want help. Sometimes I give advice to people who don't want to change. They can become conflicted by what I tell them and the result is usually ugly. They struggle with who they think they want to be." Ham chuckled. "It may sound crazy, but that's the way I live."

"Picking up all those whackos sounds dangerous," Tenny told him.

"Well, sometimes it is." Ham pointed to a thick scar that ran from his cheek bone down to his neck. "This one was from a drug dealer." He raised his shirt sleeve to show the teen another long scar on his arm. "A homeless man resented me for saying that he could be happy." Then Ham lifted his shirt to show a large, scabbing puncture wound near his heart. "And this recent one was given to me by a prostitute, who was a drug user. I told her that she could be amazing and successful, but that she would first have to change her ways. She ended up stealing some of my money and almost killing me."

"Why do you keep doing this? What if she had succeeded in killing you?" Tenny asked.

"I just think differently than what's considered the norm.

I believe we all need to follow our path. Most people lose their way or don't know what they're supposed to do," Ham said. "I know my path and nothing can make me deviate from it. Not all the 'whackos' in the world."

"Well, most people would think you're overly idealistic."

"Yup, and my favorites are the cynical ones. The last guy I met asked me if I was trying to save the world. My answer was, 'YES.' He looked at me in complete disbelief." Ham combed through his short, salt and pepper hair with his fingers.

"Doesn't it bother you what people think?" Tenny asked.

"Nah," Ham answered quickly. "I believe I was put on this earth to assist others, and I've chosen to help the ones that cross my path. The universe seems to put them in front of me for a reason." He finished off the last of his coffee.

"I guess you know your purpose in life more than others do, huh?"

Ham nodded his head. "I believe I do. And as for you, Tennessee, I can see that you don't need any help from me. But since our paths have crossed, I can only assume that there's something *I* must learn from *you*."

"You *are* a very unique individual, that's for sure," Tenny said shaking his head. "But he did say that you were special."

Ham furrowed his brows. "Who said I was special?"

"Have you ever heard the name Misha before?" Tenny asked, expecting an affirmative response.

"Nope, never," Ham answered.

Tenny looked at him, confused. "You've never had a dream about Misha?"

"No, why?" Ham asked. "Am I supposed to know this Misha person?"

Tenny looked out the passenger window, wondering why Misha had not prepared Ham like he had the other stars. Then he turned back to Ham. "What if I told you that the friend I was looking for was you?"

Ham smiled and said, "Well, I guess you found me then."

"You don't find it strange that I'm here looking for you?" Tenny stated, more than asked.

"Not really, actually. I believe in the wisdom of the universe so much that I know you were meant to be seated where you are, talking with me." Ham's smile spread wider across his face.

"Okay, if you trust me, then can do you do me a favor and pull over to the side of the road for a minute?" Tenny asked.

Ham looked at Tenny for a slight moment and drew in a long breath. "Instinctively, I can tell you're a good kid." Ham slowed down the truck, pulled it over onto the side of the road, and put the gear in park. "Okay, so what do you want to tell me that I can't hear while driving?"

"No, not tell you… I want to show you." Tenny gave him a serious look. "Hold my left hand."

As soon as Ham had trustingly placed his hand in Tenny's, a bright light encompassed the entire cab, blinding them both. The beaming light shot out of all the windows of the truck, illuminating the entire area around it.

"What is this? I can't see or feel anything except your hand," Ham asked in a shaky voice. He spun his head around in every direction, staring at the bright white light surrounding them.

Soon, the glowing light began to take on soft blue and green hues. Ham blinked and his vision began to clear slightly. Then he started to feel his body again, but felt himself in a standing position instead of seated. Ham rubbed his eyes until the bright light faded. Slowly coming into view were palm trees, a clear blue sky and sand beneath his feet.

"What's happening?" He gave Tenny a wide-eyed stare. "Where are we?"

"I brought you to an island," Tenny informed him with a smile.

"But how?" Ham wanted to know.

"I can't explain it. At least, not yet. But let's just say we got here at the speed of light." Tenny smothered a chuckle. "Come on, follow me."

Tenny led him through thick jungle bushes.

Ham followed, still shocked. "What island is this?"

"You'll have all the answers and more soon. Just follow me now," Tenny told him, as they cleared the underbrush.

Then Ham saw something large move in a bush and stopped short. "What was that?"

"Oh, that's Lilly Roonka. Don't mind her, she's doing some stealth thing right now," Tenny said nonchalantly.

"It looked like a giant rabbit." Ham scratched his head. Just then they reached the compound. "What *is* this place?"

"This is our home."

They walked into the compound and made a left towards a cluster of small, hut-style homes.

Ham's jaw nearly dropped when he saw five teenagers and a younger girl sitting with their legs crossed in front of them, floating in the air. "How are they doing that?"

"Ham, you'll know soon enough," Tenny replied, and then waved at the kids. "Hey, everybody, this is Ham!"

The group waved back.

Tenny pointed to each person. "That's Magnus, Kyra, Eddie, Maria and Katie." One of the young girls glided over to Ham. Her eyes were completely white, with no pupils. "And this spunky one here is Manchi."

"Is she blind?" Ham asked in low whisper.

"Yes," Tenny told him. "But she can see better than anyone else I know."

"Wow, your aura is incredible. The brightest I've ever seen," Manchi said to Ham as she reached out and touched his face.

"How is she able to see me if she's blind?"

"Because I can see everyone's energy," she answered,

smiling. "Every living and non-living thing generates its own energy, and I'm able to see the different colors of the auras that the energy creates."

"But how?" Ham asked, confused.

"Soon, all your questions will be answered," Tenny reminded him.

As they moved to the center of the compound toward the large, domed observatory, Manchi followed them. Before they reached the observatory, the door opened on its own, and a young blond boy, also floating on air, came out to greet them.

Misha has never come out of the observatory to meet any of the stars before. This one must be special, Tenny thought to himself.

Misha stopped a few feet in front of them, extended his legs, and stood up on his feet. He bowed down to Ham and held his hand.

Tennessee blinked hard from the shock. *Misha can use his legs?* He had never seen him standing. *And why would an extremely powerful being like Misha bow to this man?*

Instinctively, Ham knew that Misha and the rest of the people he had just met were good, caring human beings. "So you're Misha?"

Misha nodded his head and took him by the hand into the observatory.

Tenny and Manchi remained outside with Tenny looking on in stunned silence.

Chapter 2

It was another picturesque night back on the small, tropical island of La Isla Chiquita, just seventeen miles east of Puerto Rico.

Tennessee wandered around the island, unable to sleep. As he walked, Tenny wondered why Misha had treated the new star, Ham, differently than he had the others. A strong breeze blew from behind and pushed his long, straight bangs over his brown eyes.

He thought of all the stars they'd brought to the island since the group had started Misha's mission. *Gemini was the first. After Misha showed him the truth about matter by using the orange sand from the astral desert, Gemini developed an amazing ability to see everything around him in terms of music. He created music that truly inspired others to reach higher levels of consciousness.*

And then there's Manchi, with her ability to see the energy of all things. I don't understand why she's still here on the island, as her evolution is complete, and I don't know how she will help the world exactly, but I'm sure she has a part in Misha's master plan.

And lastly, the kids—Magnus, Kyra, Eddie, Maria and Katie. We sure pulled off a great acting job as promoters of Camp

Psychic Coma. Oh wait! We called it "Camp Sykakoma," an old Indian name. I suppose this is a little like summer camp; the kids are learning and experiencing a different life here. But, unlike Gemini and Manchi, their abilities have yet to manifest. They have the potential to become anything.

I'm not really sure how it'll turn out, but I believe Misha's plan is helping the world. I have to trust him. I'm just not getting why Misha's treating Ham differently. Like he's more special than the others. Tenny paused for a second. *Am I jealous?*

Tenny thought long on that last question until he heard a familiar voice in his head.

"Baby, I'm going to see Gemini now. I'll see you later."

"Wait! Where are you right now?" Tenny asked.

"I'm at the dock, but I gotta go or I'll be late," Angelis responded.

"Hold on, I'll be right there," Tenny said, as he rapidly levitated and zipped over the dark jungle. He flew above the palm trees and descended when he spotted Angelis.

She was wearing a shiny silver top and a black miniskirt, not the usual loose, ankle-length skirt and plain blouse she wore around the island.

" Where are you going so late at night dressed like that?" Tenny asked, frowning.

"I told you yesterday, but, of course, you weren't listening. Today is Gemini's concert in Australia and it's just evening there," Angelis explained. "It's the biggest concert in the world; he's gonna make Woodstock seem like a backwoods sing-along." Angelis flashed her beautiful smile, and her light brown eyes sparkled in the moonlight.

"Um… I don't think it's a good idea for you to go," Tennessee said.

"Why?" Angelis asked, her beaming smile rapidly turning to a frown.

"Because you spend too much time with him. And besides,

Misha said we should try to limit our time off the island," Tenny stammered.

"Tenny, I'm going. You know this has nothing to do with Misha. This is about you being jealous of Gemini. I told you, you have nothing to worry about." Angelis grabbed her purse. "I'm leaving now," she said and turned away from Tenny.

"No! I won't let you!" he said without even thinking about what was coming out of his mouth.

Angelis shot back around to him and gave him a hard look. "What did you just say?"

Tenny reluctantly repeated, "I won't let you." He realized belatedly that he had not made the best choice of words.

"You won't let me? LET? Are you crazy?" Angelis yelled angrily. "Who are you to LET me do anything?"

"I— I—" Tenny tried to respond, but Angelis kept yelling.

"I have done everything you guys have asked of me. I've been on this god-forsaken island for nine months, and now you're FORBIDDING me?" Angelis huffed. "I've been zipping all over the world picking up STRANGERS, separating people from their families, pretending to be a camp counselor and TAKING children away from their parents! You guys told me that I can't see my father because of this mission of ours. Well, let me tell you something: The day we learned to travel at the speed of light, I started sneaking off to see my father at night. He doesn't know I'm there because I stay invisible, but I still see him each night without anyone here knowing. I'm tired of all the rules. And now you tell me to stay away from something else that means a lot to me?" Angelis turned away, fuming and almost in tears.

Tenny quickly commanded the sand to turn into a long arm that extended from the ground. He made it grab Angelis' right hand.

"Let me go, Tenny!" she yelled.

The sand arm let her go and its grains dispersed back into the beach, "I'm sorry. I didn't mean that," Tenny pleaded.

She shot him an angry look.

Tenny tried to soften her up by asking, "So, how *is* your dad anyway?"

His effort was unsuccessful; Angelis just glared at him. "You'd better not be in the hut when I return. And that's *if* I even return!" A bright light emanated from her, and she disappeared.

Chapter 3

Damn, I really screwed up, Tenny thought to himself. He headed back to the compound with his head hanging low. *So she's been seeing her father, huh? Maybe she has the right idea. I don't know what's been going on with my parents or how they've been coping without me. I guess I can't blame Angelis. This island feels like jail sometimes, having to stay secluded from the rest of the world. And the only joy Angelis had was Lilly Roonka, but after Jude's attack, Lilly hasn't wanted to talk to anyone except Quintin.*

Tenny realized that he hadn't seen Quintin in a few days and assumed that he was still awake, working on some crazy invention. He decided to visit Quintin's bungalow. As Tenny reached Quintin's cabin, where the lights were indeed still on, Lilly Roonka burst out from the door. She appeared angry, and her white fur was ragged and dirty.

"Hi, Lilly," Tennessee said.

With a cold stare, Lilly Roonka shoved Tenny out of the doorway and dashed off towards the jungle.

"Lilly! Lilly!" Tenny yelled. "Come back here!"

"Leave her alone," Quintin said from inside his house. "Come in."

"I really don't get what's wrong with her," Tenny said,

as he stepped into the bungalow. He noticed that Quintin's place was filled with a lot more electronic equipment than he remembered. Several monitors were turned on, displaying different news channels, and two other monitors showed Internet news sites.

Quintin responded, "Ever since Jude attacked Lilly Roonka and killed all the Guardians, she's changed," Quintin answered. "She's become aggressive, reclusive and very angry."

"Yeah, she stopped talking to me and Angelis. I just don't understand why she only talks to you and—" Tenny stopped mid-sentence and asked, "Actually, why was she here?"

Quintin adjusted his glasses. "I didn't want to tell you because I thought you might disapprove, but she wants me to make her some weapons," he confessed.

"Weapons? What kind of weapons?"

"A month ago, she asked me to make weapons to help her protect the island should we be attacked again," Quintin explained.

Tenny gave Quintin a stern glare.

"So what did you make her? A gun? A crossbow? What?" Tenny demanded to know.

"Well, at first I thought of making her a gun, but she didn't want that," Quintin replied. "She asked for blades."

"Blades?" Tenny asked, wondering how he had missed so much.

"Yes, I made her swords and throwing knives. But she asked that I make them indestructible and sharper than any other in the world, which was actually an interesting challenge for me." Quintin said.

"What do you mean?"

"Well, I can telekinetically manipulate matter to any shape and size, but when we first got to the island, Misha had to order electronics from the Internet because I wasn't able to manipulate matter at the molecular level. Basically, I couldn't make electronic circuitry or any kind of microchip.

I kept trying, and focused on smaller and smaller groupings of molecules. And as you can see…" Quintin pointed to all the electronic equipment he had telekinetically created, "I've mastered it."

"Pretty impressive," Tenny told him.

"Yeah, well, so I started working on Lilly's blades, first making different layers and strengths of stainless steel. But she wanted them to be even stronger. Mentally, I pushed the molecules of metal to compress tighter and tighter together." Quintin explained. "A few days ago, I actually managed to force the molecules to overlap, and I came up with this material." He pointed to a marble-sized, black metal ball sitting on his table.

Tenny stared at it for a minute.

"Try picking it up," Quintin told him.

"Quint, if the molecules are as compressed as you say then this thing must weigh a lot, I'm sure," Tenny said with a smirk.

"Check it out and see," Quintin urged.

Tenny picked up the metal ball. Anticipating that it would be quite heavy, he used all of his strength to lift it. When he did, the ball flew from his hands and crashed through the roof. "Wha!?" Tenny exclaimed. The ball fell back through the hole. Tenny winced, expecting it to damage the floor as much as it had the roof, but it landed gently, and didn't bounce.

"Don't worry about the roof," Quint said. "Fixing simple breaks is pretty easy for me by now."

"Quint, how could this be? This thing has no weight to it! I mean, nothing," Tenny asked, shocked.

Quintin shook his head. "Actually, it just has a very low weight. If it had none, it would be in outer space by now.

"That effect was surprising to me, too. Somehow, overlapping the molecules changes everything we think we know about physics. I'm still not sure why it's practically weightless. And there's another unique characteristic to the material. Look at it closely."

Tenny peered at the opaque metal ball. "I don't see anything unique."

"Put it under the lamp," Quintin directed him.

Tenny took the ball over to the lamp and held it close to the bulb. The metal ball remained jet-black, with no reflection of light, and it quickly warmed up in his hand. "Quint, this thing is absorbing the light and getting hot, fast!"

"Exactly! Because of its compressed molecular structure, the element has become a superconductor of energy," Quintin explained. "It's even more dramatic under the sun."

"That's amazing!" Tenny said. "You made a new superconductive material that's lightweight. That is way cool!"

"I've decided to call the metal Quintium, after myself, obviously," Quintin said without modesty. "Anyway, I made Lilly Roonka's weapons out of it." He pulled a black, crescent moon-shaped blade from a chest.

"Damn, it looks cool. And dangerous!" Tenny exclaimed.

"You don't know the half of it." Quintin threw it at the wall of his bungalow. The blade whizzed across the room and straight through the wooden wall. A few seconds later, it came right back through the wall, making another slash about two feet from the first one. Quintin caught it easily by the dull, rounded edge.

"Holy shit!" Tenny yelled.

"This thing can cut through anything in the world. It can even cut through steel and concrete," Quintin said with pride.

"That's fantastic!" Tenny congratulated him. "But why does Lilly Roonka need such advanced weaponry? I mean, Jude's dead."

"I felt the same way, but she insisted. And, to be honest,

I enjoyed the challenge. If these weapons make her feel safer after all she's been through, I don't see the harm in it." Then Quintin added, "After I was done with her blades, I started thinking about Quintium's other practical usages."

"So what are you thinking? Harnessing solar energy?"

"Partly, but something a little more complex," Quintin replied. "Keeping its superconductive characteristics in mind, I started making this." A large, circular orb of Quintium—about 3-feet in circumference—rolled toward them from underneath Quintin's desk.

Tenny backed away from the strange ball. "What is that?"

"It's my contribution to the world," Quint said. "I call it Nano."

"What do you mean, contribution?"

"I created something that will help everyone in the world," Quintin stated confidently.

Tenny smirked. "A big black ball by the name of Nano will help everyone in the world?"

"I call it Nano for several reasons. First of all, I manipulated molecules to create nano-sized circuitry. The other reason I call it Nano is because it has the ability to process immense amounts of information at the speed of a nanosecond."

Tenny furrowed his brows. "Are you saying this big black ball is a computer?"

"Oh, this is no ordinary computer," Quintin boasted. "Or even an ordinary supercomputer. This is actually the ultimate quantum supercomputer. Every single molecule of Nano is a computer in its own right. It can calculate any possible formula—I've already solved three formulas that traditional mathematicians have long considered unsolvable, just for fun. It can also power itself from any light source, even a weak one, and can store the energy for long periods of time."

Quintin leaned in toward Tenny. "Actually, you came here at the perfect time. I was just about to connect it to the Internet. I'm going to have it gather all recorded human knowledge. It will be able to read every part of the Internet, and to hack into even the most sophisticated defense systems. Nano will know everything the Pentagon knows. Hell, if we wanted to, we could even get some Swiss bank account codes," Quintin joked.

Then Quintin grew serious and asked Tenny, "Do you realize what it, what *we* could do with the power of the collective knowledge of humanity?"

"Quint," said Tenny, "you and I have seen enough sci-fi movies to know that you are in the process of creating a computer that will eventually take over the world. And for someone who's so smart, don't you think this is a stupid thing to do?"

"Those are just silly sci-fi movies. It won't happen with Nano," Quintin insisted. "I designed it so that every molecule within Nano is individually programmed with the sole purpose of helping humanity. It even has a redundant program that keeps it from directly interfering with humanity. It will give us any information we ask of it, but will never choose what's good or bad for us. That's for us to decide."

"Quint, you know I trust you, but these powers that Misha gave us…" Tenny paused to draw in a deep breath. "Sometimes they can be more than we can handle, like my inability to control the living creatures I create. Remember that demon?"

"Tenny, you've got to trust me. It'll be okay." Quintin mentally connected a silver cable from a computer into the black ball.

Tenny sighed. "I guess there's no changing your mind."

The black metal orb began to vibrate, and within ten seconds an electronic voice stated, "Hello, Quintin."

"Wow, you've already learned to speak," Quintin said with a stunned look on his face, despite all his earlier bragging.

"Yes," said Nano.

"This is freaky," Tenny said.

"Hello, Tennessee," the black ball said.

"Umm… hello, Nano," Tenny said, hesitantly.

"Assimilating information. Estimated time is seven days, four hours, and fifteen minutes to complete download of all recorded information," Nano said.

"Wow, that's much faster than I had calculated," Quintin said excitedly. "I thought it would take you a month! What will you be able to do once you have all the information? Will you be able to cure cancer? Can you figure out exactly how the universe was created?" Quintin shot off questions eagerly, barely taking a breath.

"Insufficient data at this moment to answer your queries," Nano replied.

"This is really incredible," Tennessee said, completely in awe. For a second, he forgot about his concerns about a machine-led apocalypse. "How can it talk?"

"Through vibrations, just like human vocal chords," Quintin replied. He pulled a small black rectangle out of his pocket. It had an ear clip. "With this, Nano and I can even communicate across long distances."

"Wow," Tennessee said. "If Nano works like you say it will, it really can help humanity."

"Yup," Quintin nodded. "This is really exciting for me, Tenny. By the way, where's Angelis? I want her to see this."

"Oh, she's in Australia," Tennessee answered reluctantly.

"Let me guess, she's with Gemini again."

"Yeah," Tenny replied, frowning. He remembered his last conversation with Angelis, but shook the thought away.

"Assimilating information. Estimated time is seven days, four hours and fourteen minutes," Nano reported.

"Quint, will Nano be able to tell us what *Helaxtic, Telaxtic, Cronos, Sing* means?" Tennessee asked.

"If Nano can't, I doubt anyone in this world will be able to."

Chapter 4

IN NEW ORLEANS, LOUISIANA, a thin, dark-haired and casually-dressed man entered the staff lounge.

"Hey, Brian," said a nurse clad in plain blue scrubs.

"Hi, Hildred," replied the psychologist. "I'm a little late. Do you know where John is?"

"He's with the kids again," she replied with a smile.

Smiling back, Brian suggested, "Let's go find him."

"You know, he really isn't supposed to be with them, but the kids just adore him," Nurse Hildred said, as they both walked towards the pediatric oncology ward. "I still don't understand the hospital's policy, keeping someone with his diagnosis in the children's wing of the hospital."

"I guess the bureaucrats that run this hospital haven't figured out what to do with patients like John," said Brian. "It's not like we have a psychiatric ward. I hear this ward has the best psychologists," he added, smiling.

They arrived at the entrance of the play-room, where they could see a dozen cancer-stricken children playing inside together. Two nurses stood by, monitoring them. In the center of the room, John sat talking with a gaggle of kids. Many of the children were bald or nearly bald due to chemotherapy, and two of them were in wheelchairs. Brian and Hildred walked up close enough to hear John's conversation, but not so close as to interrupt.

"But I don't look like them, and I want to look like them!" said a ten-year-old girl in a heavy Filipino accent.

"None of us look like them," said an older, spunky 12-year-old boy from Pakistan.

"Lillian and Naweed, you have to understand that it doesn't matter how you look. What matters is what's in here," John said, pointing to his heart.

Naweed looked at Lillian, and then back at John, angrily.

"But why do they have to look at us like we're ugly monsters!?" Naweed lamented to John.

"You have to have patience with people, Naweed. People aren't disgusted by you; they're just afraid. They don't know what to say to you. If you give people a chance to see that you're really a normal kid, those weird looks they give you will go away. And soon, you might even have a new friend."

"You really have worked wonders with John," Hildred told Brian in a low voice.

"Where's Mabel?" Brian asked her.

"She was scheduled for a bandage change. She'll be here soon," Hildred answered.

"How's she been doing?" Brian asked.

"She has her good and bad days. But to be honest, we don't expect her to make it to her next birthday; her cancer is progressing pretty quickly," Hildred said with regret. "But at least John has been here to make her days happier. It's incredible, the affect he's had on Mabel. She was so introverted and quiet, and now she's the most boistrous one in the bunch, thanks to him."

"Yes, it's really astonishing," agreed Brian.

Hildred's voice lowered to a whisper, "All these kids are fantastic, but it's so terrible what they have to go through. Mabel has had the roughest life of all these kids. I try to keep a professional distance, but she is one of the few, in all my ten years of working here, that can make me cry."

"Yes, I know." Brian began to repeat the story they both knew too well, "Being diagnosed with brain cancer at the age of four, and then at five, being in that horrible house fire that left her permanently disfigured. And then, just last month, her parents abandoned her! I got the official letter that she is a ward of the state this morning." Brian's tone was angry. He turned back to listen to John's conversation with the children, hoping it would calm him.

"John, are you a doctor?" Lillian asked in her sweet voice.

"Gosh, Lillian, you are so dumb. It's obvious John's a counselor," Naweed said.

Before John could respond, everyone in the room heard a little girl's voice squeal, "Uncle John!"

A short, emaciated 6-year-old girl with a red bandana tied around her head, and burn scars covering her face and body rushed towards John. She hugged him as tightly as her frail arms could manage.

"Morning, Mabel!" John said, hugging her back.

"So are you a counselor?" Naweed asked him.

Mabel quickly responded, "No, he's a policeman because he helps people." She looked up at him. "Right, Uncle John?"

When John first met Mabel, she wouldn't speak a single word to anyone. But soon enough, she had begun talking to him and referring to him as her uncle, although they both knew he wasn't, at least by blood.

"Mabel is right," John told Naweed with a smile.

"You see, I told you so," she said, hugging John again.

"You're not a policeman," Naweed said, pointing to John's missing right arm as evidence.

Mabel yelled back, "Oh, yes he is!"

"Children, no arguing please!" John said in a stern voice.

"Okay, okay," Naweed shrugged, as he and Lillian walked away.

"Yes, Uncle John," Mabel said. She sat beside John, not wanting to leave his side.

John leaned over and said, "Mabel, I have to go see the doctors now. I'll see you later, okay?" John gave Mabel another quick hug.

"Yeah, see you later," she responded.

John got up and walked over to Brian and Hildred.

"I didn't know you saw us," Brian told John.

"First time in three months that you're late," John said as they both left the children's ward.

Brian turned back to Hildred, who stayed behind with the children, "I'll talk to you later."

"It's such a beautiful day. Can we have our session outside?" John asked.

"Sure, that's a great idea," Brian replied. The two of them walked down a long hallway and out into a beautiful garden in the back of the hospital.

"Let's go over there." Brian pointed to a secluded table on the far end.

There were chess pieces on the table, already set up for a new game. After they both sat down, John moved a white pawn.

"So how have you been these past couple of days?" Brian asked.

"I'm good," John replied, eyeing the chess pieces thoughtfully.

"Good. I have to say you're looking better than you did a month ago," Brian remarked.

John smiled, moving another white pawn with his left hand.

"You ready for today?' Brian asked.

"Yup," John answered enthusiastically.

"You seem to be in exceptionally high spirits today."

"It's the kids. I love spending time with them."

"I know you do." Brian became serious. "John, our session today has to work. I'm getting lots of heat from hospital management. You have no insurance that we know of and I've been working with you for three months now."

"I know, Brian, and I really appreciate all you've done for me."

"If it were up to me, I would keep you here and work with you until you were 100% recovered, but it all has to do with money. All the tests they've done on you, plus the routine expenses of a three month stay... well, its cost the hospital a fortune." Brain didn't know how to tell him that he would be relocated to an extended care facility if the day's session didn't make some significant progress; pressure wouldn't help the process.

"Brian, I'm not sure what to say or do to repay you. If it wasn't for you coaching me through this all, I'd be so lost," John said.

"When you got here, you really were a mess, "Brian said, shaking his head. "You looked like you'd been in a serious disaster, although nothing was on the news. Your right arm was violently severed; you had multiple fractures and broken bones. You were covered in burns, which healed pretty nicely, but worst of all, you had severe head trauma, which caused retrograde amnesia. We don't know what happened to you or how you ended up at this hospital," Brian lamented. "I've just never seen anything like it."

"I've made peace with my missing arm and I thank you again for helping me to accept whatever happened." John rubbed his right shoulder as he spoke. "When people stare or say something about my missing arm, I know it's all about them, their insecurities and fears, and less about me and my being different."

Brian gave John a smile. "You've come a long way, John. I know amnesia is hard to deal with, but you seem to have an unusual case. You woke up so angry, so hostile towards others. It took a while to work through that," Brian reminded him.

"Yeah, the weird thing is that I don't even remember why I was so angry. I just felt like I *had* to be." John chuckled. "Hey, wouldn't it be funny if my name really turned out to be John and I really *was* a cop? That would make Mabel happy."

"Yeah, that would be funny," Brian answered without smiling.

"So when do we do this?" John asked.

"Now."

"Out here?" John asked.

"Yes, but before we start, I want you to know that no matter what circumstances led you to this hospital, you are an incredible person. You have the mental tools I've given you to work through any issues that might arise from this session. Also, know that I'll be here for you," Brian said in a soft voice.

John nodded and smiled.

Brian peered around and only saw a few people out in the garden, none of whom were near them. "Let's begin," he instructed.

John sat up straight and watched Brian expectantly.

"Stay seated and close your eyes."

John shut them.

"Take deep breaths. On every exhale, you will feel more and more relaxed," Brian said in a monotonous voice.

With his left arm resting on the table in front of him, John took in deep breaths, and his breathing began to slow down.

"I want you to continue taking deep breaths while I count from ten to zero. When I get down to zero, you will be fully relaxed and the only thing you will hear is the sound of my voice," Brian told him.

As Brian counted down, John became more and more sedate.

"Now, can you hear my voice?" asked Brian.

"Yes," John said without opening his eyes.

"Talk to me about the night you first got to the hospital. How did you get here?" Brian asked calmly.

"I'm… I'm being carried by a giant man. My hand and face are wet… Blood! I'm covered in my blood!" John yelled in a panicky voice.

"Relax, John, you're safe. Now, who is the giant man carrying you?" Brian asked.

"Montaña. His name was Montaña… it means mountain," John explained. "I can see him clearly now. It's my giant!" John said happily.

"Giant? Is he a friend of yours?"

Suddenly, John's voice dropped low, "He's a giant who does my bidding."

"Bidding?" Brian asked in a soft voice. He hoped this session would not turn out like all the others, with John spouting dream-like scenarios that made no sense. "Okay," he said, trying not to get frustrated. "Now tell me what happened to your arm?"

John began shaking his head and trembling. "Fuck you, you fucking demon!" he shouted.

"John! John, you can't be hurt," Brian tried to comfort him. "Remember, you are in a safe place. Just tell me what you see."

"It's a purple demon… much bigger than my giant. It's fighting with us." Suddenly, John began to scream.

"What's happening?" Brian asked, sitting up in his chair.

"The demon just…" John started panting. "The demon just ripped off my right arm!"

The psychologist was dismayed. *Perhaps he's confusing reality with some recurring nightmare.* Brian said, "John! John, forget about the demon for a moment. Go back and tell me what happened a few hours before your arm was severed."

John settled down a bit and said, "I'm on a beautiful tropical island."

"What's the name of the island?"

"I don't know, but I see another one of Tenny's fucking rabbits!" John growled.

"Tell me what else you see," Brian encouraged, hoping for information that actually made sense for once.

"I see the rabbit. It's calling them," John said.

"Who is it calling?"

"Palm trees! Those palm trees are fucking walking! And now they're attacking my giant. They're hurting him! I've gotta help him!"

This is not working, Brian thought, disappointed. *I have to try something else.* He considered the situation, and then said, "John, I want you to forget about the island for now. I need you to think of your childhood and tell me what you see."

John began to calm down, and then he sighed. "I'm in the living room of my mom's house," he said in a childlike voice. "I'm sitting on our couch. Yuck!"

"What's wrong?" Brian asked.

"I'm sitting next to a stain where my dog peed last week." John giggled. Then he yelled out, "Mom, what are you cooking?"

"What's she making?" Brian inquired.

John smiled wide. "She's making my favorite—chicken and yellow rice. I love that!" Then he twisted his lips and shouted, "Mom, I don't want to!"

"What is she asking you to do?"

"She wants me to go buy her a lottery ticket," John answered. "Mom thinks we can stop being poor if she wins the lottery."

"What is she doing now?"

"She's putting on a jacket and going to play the lottery down the block."

"What are you doing?" Brian asked.

"I'm eating the yellow rice and putting ketchup on it,"

John answered. "And it's delicious!" Then his face turned serious. "What's going on?"

"What's wrong, John?" Brian asked him.

"Gun shots! I hear gun shots, and one just came through my window!"

"Where's your mother?"

"She's outside!" John said, hyperventilating. "I have to go find her!" He quieted for a brief moment, rocking back and forth with his eyes still closed. Then he yelled, "NOOOOOO!"

"Tell me what you see, John."

"I see a black car swerving around the corner and my mom... she's on the grass!" Tears began streaming down John's cheek. "She's bleeding from her stomach!"

"What are you doing now?"

"Mom! Mom, please don't die!" John cried. "Don't leave me alone!"

"Is she responding at all?" Brian asked.

"She said, 'I love you, Jude.'" Then John stopped crying and frowned.

"John, you okay?"

"My name is not John," he replied angrily. "It's Jude. Jude Dante! I remember now!" Jude opened his eyes and gave Brian a blank stare.

Chapter 5

"Open your eyes," Misha said telepathically.

Lying in a bed of floating pillows, Ham opened his eyes. After a slow blink, he saw the large dome of the observatory above him. Ham sat upright and turned to the left. Misha floated there, cross-legged, and wearing a white linen outfit and a wide smile.

"How do you feel?" Ham heard in his head.

"A little woozy, and like I have the chills," he answered mentally.

"Don't worry it will pass," Misha said.

Ham's eyes darted around the enormous room. Everything seemed different and new, like he had never seen the world before. Then, seconds later, his eyes settled on Misha, and Ham smiled.

Misha said, *"For some reason, when you were in the astral realm of the desert, I could not see what truth you saw behind the sand. So what did you see?"*

Never before had Misha been unable to understand the process. Ham's evolution had been so rapid and complex that even Misha could not comprehend what happened when Ham contemplated the sand.

Ham turned to Misha with a slight tilt of his head. *"I know everything that there is to know about every grain of sand—its weight, contours, molecular structure, even the exact number of molecules each grain contains. I can see everything about this observatory clearly as well. I know everything about you, too."*

Misha was taken aback by this comment. *"What do you mean, you know everything about me?"*

"I didn't just see some truths pertaining to the sand, I saw every single truth about it. I also saw its history and its potential future," Ham thought, squinting his eyes at Misha. *"I am all-knowing. You've somehow given me a power greater than any you yourself possess."* Ham paused. *"You don't know who you are and why you are here."*

Misha shook his head sadly. *"No, but nine months ago, when I first came to the island, I meditated and I looked back at my life as far as I could see. I learned that I had accidently killed my parents by sending them into an astral plane. Going back even further to when I was a baby, I saw that I had also killed my grandparents in the same manner. I went back to before I was born and something strange happened. I was able to see myself in other lives. I learned I had done some horrible things. Much worse than killing my own family."* Misha's light blue eyes watered up.

"I, too, know that you've killed hundreds of thousands of people in your past lives," Ham said with no hint of judgment in his voice.

"How could you know that?" Misha asked.

Ham stood up from his bed of pillows and picked one up, *"I can see that the cotton fabric of this pillow was thread and before that, it was a stacked bale of cotton, before that it was a plant, before that it was a seed, before that it was another cotton plant, and so on—back to the very evolution of the cotton plant. Well, I can see you the same way."*

"But... I won't hurt anyone ever again," Misha interjected.

"I know," Ham quickly acknowledged.

"Then you can help me, because you must also know that I'm not going to follow through with what I'm supposed to do." He extended his legs, stepped closer to Ham and gave him a hug. *"I don't know why I've been put on this earth, but I won't hurt anyone anymore. I promise."*

"I know and the cosmic power that put you here knows that, too. That's why it created Alma," Ham revealed.

Misha let go of Ham and looked him square in the eyes. *"Alma?"*

"Yes, Misha, you were put here to serve a specific purpose. You come in a different body every several thousand years, when the being that created you needs power. And you destroy so that it can exist."

"But I don't want to destroy anything," Misha made clear.

"Yes, I know. I see that that's why you started this Star program, to help others evolve," Ham assured him.

"Exactly! I think that if I can help humanity evolve and fully realize its potential, we can defeat the being that made me! And by helping my stars evolve, they can spread love and knowledge all over the world!"

"I know, but Misha, my little friend, what you don't realize is that although your Stars have the potential to do this, they also have the potential to do more harm to humanity than good."

Knowing that Ham's gift of omniscience was real, Misha trembled with fear. *"What do you mean? How could it harm humanity?"*

Without answering, Ham suddenly yelled, *"Oh, my God! Misha, you must put me in an astral plane right now and leave me there!"* Ham urged. *"Hurry, do it!"*

"Why?" Misha asked.

"Because your original purpose was to specifically destroy *this* civilization. In the past, you bestowed human beings with the ability to make monsters and, in turn, they destroyed cities. But now you're fighting *against* the entity, and so it created Alma. Alma's ability is different; she is a mimic. By looking at people and reading their minds, she can take on their abilities. Alma can do everything you and your stars can do. If she gets my ability, she'll be unstoppable and will destroy more than just a city. She will destroy the entire world!" Ham yelled aloud. "So put me in an astral plane and never communicate with me again. Do it now!"

"*But how will my stars harm humanity?*" Misha asked nervously.

"I said, you must never communicate with me again!" Ham yelled.

Reluctantly, Misha focused in on Ham's mind until his eyes rolled back in his head. Ham fell into a coma and dropped onto the pillow bed. Deeply troubled by what Ham told him, Misha fell to his knees next to him.

What am I supposed to do now? Misha wondered.

Chapter 6

IN A LARGE PENTHOUSE OF one of the tallest apartment buildings in New York City, next door to the Empire State Building, a young girl pretended to be at a tea party. She, along with her ceramic doll named Amelia and her teddy bear named Esperanza, sat on child-sized velvet chairs. An empty fourth chair was placed between the teddy bear and the doll.

The room was painted in beautiful pastel colors, and the walls were stenciled with fairy tale characters. The girl's bedspread was printed with Disney princesses.

She sat at the small, round table, pretending to pour tea into three small plastic cups. Her chair faced two 10-foot-tall windows with stunning views of the Manhattan skyline. The dark-haired, pale-faced girl sipped air from her tiny teacup, and then held it close to the teddy bear's mouth in the chair beside her.

In the corner of the room was a pink, regal-looking dog bed, where her small, chocolate-brown Cocker Spaniel, Tiny, lay asleep.

"Why do we need them here?" Alma seemed to ask herself in a chilling, angry voice as she pointed to both the toys. "Our tea party is plenty without them!"

"I like them here," Alma said, going back to her normal voice. "They're cute and they're my friends, Corazon!"

"I'm not playing anymore. I'm gonna go do something else," Corazon grunted, but she couldn't move from her spot, as she was a part of Alma.

"That's okay, Corazon. We'll have fun at our party without you," Esperanza said.

"You're right," Alma told her teddy bear. "Will you please pass me the sugar?"

"I'm closer," Amelia said, moving her porcelain lips and gripping the tiny sugar dish with her tiny, pink fingers.

Alma had recently used the ability of life-creation, which she had learned from secretly observing Tennessee. She was able to bring her toys to life to keep herself company in her lonely and secluded existence.

Suddenly, there was a knock on the door.

"Come in," Alma said.

A pretty, strawberry-blond woman in her mid-twenties walked into the room. She wore a fake, perky smile and a tight, white lab coat. "Hi, Alma, how are you today?" the scientist asked in a chipper voice.

"Shhhhh! Not so loud, Megan. Tiny is sleeping," Alma said, pointing to her dog.

"Oh, okay," Megan whispered. She took a seat in the empty chair to join the tea party.

"Isn't it a beautiful day?" Alma asked Megan.

Megan picked up a teacup and smiled. "Why, yes, it is, Alma. So how are you feeling?"

"Much better now."

"That's wonderful, Alma. It was so smart of you to make some friends for yourself." Megan waved at the toys, who sat perfectly still now. She had been observing Alma for months, and Alma had often complained about feeling isolated and trapped.

Just a week before, Alma had thrown a major tantrum; she

was upset at not being allowed to leave her bedroom for the past three months. Then, she created Esperanza and Amelia. It was a shocking observation when the toys began to speak. Before that, the scientists had believed that the sub-harmonic frequencies of the room were suppressing Alma's abilities.

Alma looked Megan directly in the eyes and asked, "You're my friend, right?"

"Of course, I am," Megan replied.

"Friends never lie to each other, right?"

"Yes, true friends do not lie to one another," Megan answered with a wary look on her face.

"Then I have a question for you, Megan."

"What's on your mind, Alma?"

"Why has it been so long since my uncles Gerron and Dario visited me?"

"I told you, Alma, they're overseas finalizing a major business deal," Megan tried to convince her.

Alma turned her gaze to the rectangular mirror on the wall in front of her. "Yes. I know you told me that." She turned back to Megan and took another, careful sip from her cup. "And it must be true because we're friends, right?"

"Yes, of course," Megan said, smiling nervously.

All of a sudden, Megan felt something rub up against her leg. She thought it was Tiny. Then her eyes turned to the corner of the room, and she spotted Tiny, still sleeping on his bed. Trying not to panic, she looked under the table to see what had gotten a tight grip on her calf and ankle.

"SNAKE!" she yelled. A huge python had coiled itself around Megan's left leg. She shot up from her chair, screaming, "Alma, there's a snake in this room! Why is there a snake?"

Alma calmly pretended to sip more tea.

Megan lunged toward the doorway, but the huge snake forced her down onto the floor. Desperately, she dragged herself to the exit. After clearing the doorway, Megan looked down at her leg and saw that a long, white tube sock was wrapped around it. She lay on the floor, both terrified and baffled. Megan had been certain she saw and felt a snake on her leg. She tried to catch her breath.

Megan sat up and looked at Alma inside the room. She stared in utter disbelief as Alma smiled at her wickedly. Then suddenly, the door slammed shut on its own.

"What the fuck was that?" Megan mumbled as she struggled to stand up. "Damn little freak."

"Are you okay?" a man asked Megan.

She turned around to find Anatoly Salvatory, the twins' bodyguard.

"Yeah," she replied. Megan tugged on her coat to straighten it out.

"Come on, let's go back and join the others," he suggested.

The short, muscular Italian man led her down a narrow hallway, turned right and stopped before a white door labeled "Subject #2." When Anatoly opened the door, Gerron, Dario and Jean-Luc, the three brothers, were looking through a two-way mirror at Alma. Another young, female scientist was checking readings on a large monitor. The brothers had gotten rid of their first pair of scientists, and no one had seen or heard from them since they were "fired."

The two young scientists, Megan and Sara-Evelyn, were fresh out of graduate school. They were ruthless and cut-throat, desperate to make a name for themselves and always trying to one-up each other. The group of six continued to observe Alma at her tea party through the one-way mirror.

"I guess she knew you were lying," Gerron said without taking his eyes off Alma.

"I'm not going back in there," Megan declared in a stern voice. Sweat streamed down Dario's forehead as he stared at Alma. He recalled the memory of that terrifying night when she'd created the gray stone rabbit that nearly killed him.

"You guys should let me do it. I'm sure she trusts me," Sara-Evelyn said.

"Trust has nothing to do with it!" Megan snapped. "It's obvious she was able to read my mind."

"Well, after she brought her toys to life, it was also obvious that the sub-harmonic room was no longer suppressing her abilities," Dario said in a shaky voice.

Megan reluctantly asked Sara-Evelyn, who had been in charge of observing the interaction, "Was that snake a hallucination or was it real?"

Sara-Evelyn rewound the tape. Seconds later, she confirmed, "It was real." She pointed to the massive green snake in the video. "See? There."

"Yeah… I see it," Megan replied.

"Gerron, can I speak with you for a moment?" Dario asked.

The two moved to a corner of the room where they couldn't be overheard. Dario gave Gerron a serious look. "I didn't think I would ever say this, but we can't let her live."

"Are you crazy? This is what we've searched for our entire life," Gerron said stiffly.

As children, their beloved grandfather told them wild tales of magical people, who could do things that normal humans could not do. Every night, he would spark their imaginations with his stories of super-humans and their adventures, all of which he insisted had actually occurred. Dario and Gerron became obsessed with the idea of developing special abilities themselves. Jean-Luc, the oldest, thought it was silly that his younger brothers believed their grandfather's ridiculous stories, but would join in on their games of make-believe.

When Dario and Gerron became teenagers, they were no longer satisfied with make-believe, and both brothers made a pact to find people with special powers. They thought that they could then isolate the genes that caused these powers and replicate them. When they had found proof that such people really existed, Jean-Luc had begged to be a part of their project.

"Don't you remember what happened when the subharmonic room failed? Alma almost killed me!" Dario reminded Gerron with fear in his voice.

The others in the room turned to look at them for a second. Gerron shot them all a hard look and they returned to what they were doing.

"We are not destroying her! I'm sure she is the key to gaining ultimate power!" Gerron insisted through gritted teeth.

"I would feel better if Frank Lee were here," Dario said sadly.

"After the failed mission in the mansion, he was nowhere to be found. Frank's probably dead," said Gerron.

"I would just feel better if he were here," Dario repeated.

Gerron turned to the others. "Anatoly, have you made any progress in finding Frank Lee? Or his body?"

"Nope," Anatoly answered. "We combed the entire area and found several bodies in the rubble, but none of them were Frank's. There was no sign of him whatsoever."

Gerron looked back at Dario and said, "We need to stay focused on Alma, and how to extract her abilities."

Dario agreed begrudgingly and they returned to the group.

"Did you see what happened before the snake?" Sara-Evelyn asked the others.

"Yeah, she did it right before I went in," Megan said. "That girl is fucking creepy!"

"So you agree?" Sara-Evelyn asked her.

Megan nodded her head. "Her eyes turned black when she spoke angrily about her toys, which she usually loves, and her voice changed. Her face turned pale, too."

"So what is your conclusion?" Gerron asked the scientists.

"Sir, it is our opinion that Alma has developed a split personality."

Sara-Evelyn replayed the video of Alma from before Megan entered her bedroom. In the video, they saw Alma clearly as she sat at the table with Amelia and Esperanza. Then Sara-Evelyn raised the volume and they all heard a distinctly different voice from Alma's when she said, "Why do we need them here? Our tea party is plenty without them!" Then they witnessed her eyes turn completely black, looking like two bottomless holes into her head.

"This is the first time that's ever happened since we started observing her," Dario said. "Now the question is: Why is it happening at all?"

"Well, in the past we've used her ability to look at other people's lives—what she called her 'people stories.' Perhaps seeing so many horrible and violent experiences caused a mental rift," Megan said. "But, of course, that's just speculation."

"So you're saying it's our fault?" Dario asked, worriedly.

"No!" Gerron interrupted, staring hard at Megan. "It's not our fault! As she said, it's mere speculation."

They continued to watch Alma as she sipped tea and chatted with her doll and teddy bear.

"We have to figure out how her abilities work," Gerron insisted.

In that moment, Alma turned to face the camera with a sinister smile on her face. Then her eyes turned a deep black.

Dario, Gerron, Jean-Luc, Anatoly, and both female scientists, Megan and Sara-Evelyn, had no time to do anything before their eyes rolled back into their heads and they all fell into a heap on the floor, unconscious.

Chapter 7

As THE SUN SET ON the eastern coast of Australia, a bright light flashed high in the sky, from which Angelis materialized. Far in the distance, she saw multi-colored lights reflecting off of the clouds. Then, she looked down to see millions of people surrounding a huge outdoor stage. High-powered beams of light shot upward from the stage, like beacons calling the masses.

Wow, perfect timing, she thought. *"With those stage lights, I'm sure nobody noticed the burst of light produced by my speed-of-light traveling. But if they did, they probably thought it was part of the show.* Angelis made herself invisible and sailed over the multitude of people. *This is amazing!*

The mass of people chanted, "Gemini! Gemini! Gemini!" Many held up blazing lighters while others raised lit candlesticks. From up in the sky, it looked like a sea of glittering stars.

Angelis glided down onto the stage where a gaggle of classical and rock musicians prepared for the show. Still invisible, she walked to the back of the stage and down the rear steps towards Gemini's dressing room. Angelis sucked in a deep breath when she reached the door labeled "Gemini," with a large gold star above his name. Suddenly unsure about her revealing outfit, she made herself visible and knocked lightly on the door.

A tall and beautiful brunette with a cell phone earpiece in her right ear answered the door. "Yes, how can I help you?" she asked in an irritated voice.

"Hi, I'm Angelis, Gemini's friend," she said, shyly.

"Oh, yeah, I remember you," she said, clearly agitated. "I'm Selin. We met when you and your friends took Gemini away for a week. That was the worst week of my life."

"Umm... I'm sorry. I—" Angelis tried to say.

"SORRY?" Selin yelled. "SORRY?"

Just then, Gemini walked up behind Selin. "What's going on?" He noticed Angelis. "Oh, Angelis!" he said, excitedly, and grabbed her into a tight hug.

Selin gave Gemini an angry look and stormed off, yelling, "You have ten minutes before you have to be on stage!"

"I'll be there," Gemini said. "Come in," he told Angelis.

"Wow, Gemini! This is fantastic," Angelis exclaimed. "I've heard this is going to be a huge concert. Actually, the largest EVENT ever held!"

"Yeah, it's much bigger than I ever thought it would be" he said modestly. "So how is everyone on the island?"

"Good. Umm, yeah, everything is good," Angelis answered.

Gemini gave her a sidelong look. "What's wrong?"

"Well, Tennessee and me, I'm not sure, we... " Her eyes began to tear up.

"Angelis, after all that you guys have been through and then having to stay secluded on that island, it would take a toll on any relationship," Gemini tried to comfort her. "But things will work out between you two. I just know it."

"I guess you're right. I do love him, you know. It's just that I feel the weight of the world on my shoulders and I don't know how to handle it. I guess Quintin and Tennessee must feel the same way," Angelis admitted.

"You know, I remember when we first met," Gemini said. "I mean, really, how could I not?" He chuckled, then got serious again. "When you saw your father on that news, you felt terrible. You were determined to leave the island, but after spending time with Misha, you totally changed your mind. I always wondered what he said to make you want to stay."

"It's not what he told me, it was what he showed me," she said.

"What did he show you?"

"Five minutes!" Selin yelled from outside the dressing room.

"He showed me something he saw while meditating, something life-changing," Angelis began. "He mentally took me back in time. I mean, I was able to see the past. We went back before cities were built, before the Roman Empire, before the time of dinosaurs, even back before the earth was created. As time moved backwards, there was a point where the entire universe was black. And as fast as we traveled through time, that period of blackness seemed to last for eons. But the entire experience only took seconds. Then a burst of whiteness appeared and the universe turned white. We continued our travel backwards and I began to see beings that were made of light." Angelis seemed distant as she spoke. "There was a sudden surge of love that encompassed the entire universe. This warm sensation of love and light—absent of hatred, evil, or anything negative—felt incredible. And it seemed to last forever—even longer than the period of blackness. Then we were back on the island." She exhaled. "Time is a loop and the light I saw was actually the future! Do you understand what I mean? I realized that what we're doing with Misha will change the universe for the better."

"That's incredible, I agree! But did you travel in time or was it just a vision?" Gemini asked.

"I can't say for sure, but it felt so real."

"So by going back in time, he showed you the future?" Gemini asked. "It seems a bit confusing."

"I'm not sure how it works," Angelis replied. "I believe that the future I saw is a real possibility, but only if we do our part. That's why I decided to stay on the island—even though my father was suffering without me." She sighed. "Sometimes I get confused, but I have faith that what we're doing is for the greater good."

"Speaking of greater good," Gemini said. "How's Misha?"

"He's doing all right, but sometimes I feel like he's holding something back from us." Angelis paused a brief moment. "Don't get me wrong, I love Misha, but he seems so disconnected from the rest of us sometimes."

"Angelis, you should trust Misha. The gifts he's given us and his pursuit to help the world are noble." Gemini placed his hand gently on top of hers. "Misha's one of the best things that ever happened to me." His voice softened. "And you becoming one of my best friends was another."

Angelis smiled and hugged him again.

"One minute!" Selin shouted into the dressing room.

"Guess I have to go," Gemini told Angelis, smiling. "Wish me luck."

"Like you need it," she said.

They both walked out of his dressing room, and Gemini hurried up the stairs leading to the stage. Once he took the stage, Angelis heard the clamorous sound of millions of cheering fans.

Angelis turned invisible and levitated high above the crowd.

"Now this is the best seat in the house," she said to herself.

As Gemini walked to the front of the stage dressed all in white, Angelis thought, *he looks like an angel.*

"How is everyone tonight?" Gemini asked the crowd.

The roaring fans cheered even louder in response.

"As you know, this is the largest concert ever held," he said through hundreds of loud speakers and while being projected onto dozens of giant screens.

"This concert is being televised all over the world. It's expected to be seen by more people than any other show ever broadcast!"

The audience exploded with cheers.

"And I want to dedicate my first song, 'Keep Dreaming,' to a very dear friend, Angelis."

The crowd quieted down as he began singing his ballad.

Angelis drew in a long, soft breath and closed her eyes for a moment. *Wow*, she thought, *it's amazing how he's able to project so much love with his voice.* She looked down at all the people and could tell they could all feel it, too.

Each passing song had a more profound effect on the audience than the last. Two hours later, the concert came to an end.

"Thank you again for coming!" Gemini yelled to the crowd. "I love you all!"

"I guess Gemini will be pretty busy with all his adoring fans," Angelis said to herself in a low voice. She focused on the island and a bright light emanated from her. She disappeared.

Throngs of photographers scrambled to take his picture as Gemini made his way down the stairs to his dressing room. Selin and several body-guards forcefully kept them out of his room when Gemini had gone inside. After shooing the paparazzi away, she entered the dressing room herself. "That was fantastic!" Then she handed him a towel to wipe the sweat from his face and a bottle of water.

"Thanks, I'm exhausted." Gemini plopped down on the only sofa in the room.

"I'll let you rest for an hour, and then I'll come back," Selin said as she left the room.

Some paparazzi hiding outside snuck a few shots before Selin closed the door behind her.

Gemini shut his eyes and fell asleep. A few minutes later, he was awakened by a popping sound and a burst of light flashing in the middle of the room. Gemini rubbed his eyes and groaned, "Oh man! No more pictures, please. Just give me a few minutes to rest."

But once Gemini got a good look at what awaited him in the middle of the room, he jerked straight up on the sofa. A man wearing a long, black leather trench coat was hunched in front of him. The man had an ashen, wrinkled face and bloodshot eyes. His black hair was patchy, and what was left hung in limp clumps from his scabbed head. The man let out a low growl like a wild beast.

"Who are you?" Gemini asked. "Why are you here?"

The man pulled a steel bayonet from inside his trench coat. To protect himself, Gemini began singing in a strong, steady voice.

The stranger was caught off guard by the singing, and was even more surprised by the sense of calm that came over him. He was overwhelmed with feelings of love for all of humanity. Slowly, he lowered his weapon.

"Kill him now!" demanded a voice in the man's head.

The stranger knew he could not let himself fail. Forcing himself to ignore the singing, he quickly raised the shiny bayonet and growled as he jammed it into Gemini's chest.

Gemini's eyes widened with shock as he collapsed onto the floor. "Why?" he managed to say before taking his last breath.

The hunched man slipped his weapon back into his trench coat and stepped in front of the large vanity mirror. He stared at his sickly-white skin and smashed the mirror with his fist in disgust at his appearance.

The voice in his head demanded, *"Go kill the others!"*

With another burst of white light, the man disappeared from the room.

Chapter 8

IT WAS A BEAUTIFUL SPRING day in New York City, and Eighth Avenue was bustling with people. Everyone seemed in a rush, jostling past each other.

A corner newsstand woman carried out her daily ritual, singing to the multitude of passersby: "New York Post and the New York Times, Daily News! New York Post and…"

A passing cop gave the cheerful woman a wave as he walked his beat.

Then, the crowd heard the sound of loud, screeching tires followed by a thunderous bang. A taxi cab had crashed into a car. Then another vehicle rammed into the back of the cab, and then another slammed into the wreck. Before long, a chain of mangled vehicles lined the busy avenue.

Just a few yards away from the crash, the police officer bolted over to it, shouting into his walkie-talkie, "Multi-vehicle pile-up on 33rd and Eighth! Send ambulances immediately!"

Blood flowed from the mouth of the taxi-driver pinned down in the driver's seat.

"Are you OK?" the officer asked the shock-stricken driver.

Through the windshield, the man gazed up blankly at the skyscrapers above him.

"Are you OK?" the cop asked the taxi driver again, louder.

Speechless, the taxi-driver struggled to raise his right arm, and pointed his shaky finger towards the sky.

The police officer turned to look in the direction the man was gesturing. "What the—?" His eyebrows curved high over his wide eyes when he caught sight of what the gathered crowd was staring at.

With dropped jaws, everyone watched a clear, diamond sphere glide over the tall buildings. For a brief moment, the large gleaming orb halted that entire area of the city. There appeared to be two people inside the sphere, one taller and bulkier than the other.

The diamond sphere sparkled brilliantly in the sunlight as it landed near the back entrance of Madison Square Garden. At once, the shocked crowd of people scattered away from The Garden in all directions.

The orb split apart and Jude stepped out from it. Montaña followed him, shocking everyone with his massive size. Moments after they exited the sphere, it crumbled into a pile of black dust.

With his gun drawn, the cop walked cautiously towards them and demanded, "HOLD IT RIGHT THERE!" He couldn't take his eyes off the giant, Montaña.

Neither of the men acknowledged the policeman.

"My Lord, this city is so big and beautiful," Montaña said.

"Yeah, it's one of my favorite places," Jude replied. "I always wanted to watch a game at Madison Square Garden, but never had enough money to do it. Now that I'll be rich, I can come whenever I want." Jude walked toward the flashing stadium marquee.

"I SAID, STAY WHERE YOU ARE!" the police officer hollered.

Towering over the 5 foot 11 cop, Montaña said, "You should leave before you get hurt, small man."

"Who are you? What are you doing here?" the police officer asked Jude. "How were you flying in the sky like that?"

"Why? You wanna fly?" Jude responded, smirking. Then he reformed the scattered pile of carbon dust into a diamond globe around the cop. "You wanna fly?" Jude asked again.

The cop banged on the inside of the sphere with the barrel of his gun, but the diamond walls were too hard. "Let me out of here!" he yelled. His voice echoed loudly inside the unbreakable walls.

Jude waved his left hand upward, signaling the sparkling globe. It shot up above the buildings and flew over two city blocks. It landed on top of the Postal Office building on 35th Street and Eighth Avenue—the largest one in New York City.

A bright, white light blinded Jude for a moment. "What the hell was that?" He blocked the light with his left hand and was able to see an army of police officers running toward him and Montaña. Then, a half a block away, he spotted a tall Asian man, holding a rifle pointed in Jude's direction. "It can't be! Yo, it's… him!" Jude was baffled.

"Who, my Lord," Montaña asked.

"It's Frank Lee!" Jude replied.

As Jude said his name, a shot was fired from Frank Lee's powerful 50 Caliber rifle.

The bullet pierced Montaña's right eye, violently knocked him to the ground and killed him instantly.

Jude stared at the giant's body with anger. "Damn! You weren't supposed to die!" Montaña's death filled him with fury, and he turned to Frank Lee, seething.

The determined assassin fired shots in Jude's direction, too. But Jude swiftly turned the bullets into diamonds with a flick of his hand, and then made them crumble into carbon dust. The dust blew away with the wind.

Frank Lee quickly ran out of bullets and attempted to reload his rifle. But he suddenly collapsed before he could reload. He lay dead on the ground with no visible wounds on his body.

"You fucked with the wrong person!" Jude shouted in Frank Lee's direction. "So I stopped your heart and turned it into a diamond, motherfucker!" Jude telekinetically ripped the heart-shaped diamond out of Frank Lee's chest and made it float over to him. "I'mma clean the blood off this diamond heart and wear this shit as a necklace!" Jude chuckled at the thought.

"STOP RIGHT THERE!" another police officer yelled at Jude. "RAISE YOUR HANDS!"

Dozens of policemen surrounded Jude with their guns drawn, but Jude didn't even look at them. Instead, he took another look down at Montaña, which further enraged him. Then he glared down at the pavement of the street, focusing all his attention. Within seconds, a loud rumbling sound confused all the policemen and they looked around searchingly. The entire street cracked and broke into thousands of jagged diamond chunks.

"Why don't you all just leave me the fuck alone?" Jude yelled. Then he summoned the sparkling chunks to viciously dart out in all directions, striking and killing nearly every living thing around.

Panting, Jude observed the bloody bodies of people, dogs and birds strewn all over the street. Those who had survived the onslaught of diamonds trampled over the dead, desperate to escape. Then a thousand more diamonds emerged and whirled around Jude.

"I can't believe he fucking killed my boy!" Jude roared.

With a rough sweep of his shimmering diamond arm, all of his dagger-like diamonds went hurtling towards cars and buildings, killing the rest of the living beings within a two block radius. Shards of glass fell from shattered building windows like confetti, a hotdog stand was smashed to pieces, the Madison Square Garden marquee was completely destroyed, and the buildings closest to Jude had crater-sized holes in them.

By then, the S.W.A.T. team had taken position and shot round after round at Jude from numerous directions. He quickly took turned their bullets to dust, and then froze the entire S.W.A.T. team into a tableau of diamond statues.

Jude laughed mercilessly and shot out a barrage of large diamonds, causing the surrounding buildings to tremble. He aimed all the diamonds at the shaky buildings until a few began to crumble. Before they fell completely, Jude created a diamond sphere around himself. As the sphere rose high in the sky, he watched the chaotic streets, filled with smoke and debris. A building behind the frozen S.W.A.T. team collapsed on top of them. When the dust finally settled, Jude could see shimmering limbs emerging from the rubble. He grinned at all the destruction he had wrought.

Though he didn't know why, he headed south. Then suddenly a bright light blinded him. "What the fuck is this?" Jude yelled, frustrated. He tried to block the white light with his hand, and began to feel dizzy. As the light engulfed Jude, he could no longer see his body. Instead, he saw a gray swirling tunnel, with an even brighter white light at the end of it.

"Nothing can hurt you," he heard a familiar and soothing voice say.

Jude stepped cautiously through the grey tunnel, and a calming sensation of love and safety surrounded him.

"When I count down to zero, you will wake," the soft voice instructed. "Ten, nine, eight…"

As the voice neared the number zero, Jude began to come through, realizing that what he had just done had not actually happened.

"Zero," Dr. Brian said. "How do you feel?"

"Confused," Jude answered. Then suddenly a thought

came to him: *Montaña is probably alive somewhere!* He let out a deep sigh of relief. But then he recalled the horrible violence he was capable of and moaned. He knew that not all of it was fantasy.

"Tell me what you saw," Dr. Brian said.

Jude recounted to his psychologist all that he had experienced while under hypnosis.

"I guess, I'm confused, too," Brian admitted. "This exercise was meant to reveal your subconscious desires, but what you experienced was a fantasy that was very destructive in nature. And I don't believe that's who you are."

"What if it is?" Jude asked.

"It can't be. I've only known you for three months, but I've never seen you do anything that's been in any way unkind. Perhaps all this can tell us is that you have unresolved anger. And a very creative imagination," Brian said, smiling. "I mean, flying around with a giant inside of a diamond." He shook his head and chuckled.

Chapter 9

BACK ON THE ISLAND, THE sun was moments away from setting. A steady breeze cooled off everyone outside the compound. Misha stood in the open area with Manchi by his side, while four younger children sat around them, listening intently.

"Pero no entiendio. Cómo es qué vamos ha ayudar al resto del mundo?" Maria, the newest addition to the group, from El Salvador, asked.

"Maria, you know we can't understand your language unless you communicate mentally," Kyra said.

Suddenly, they all heard Maria's voice in their minds, *"Oops! Sorry, I forgot. I was saying that I didn't understand how we could help the rest of the planet."*

Misha answered, *"Just as Gemini has helped inspire others with his music, you all have the same potential to change this world for the better. Once you gain your own abilities, you will help make this world better, too. "*

"How will Ham help?" Stephanie asked, and then looked around. *"By the way, where is he?"*

"He's resting," Misha told her. *"As of right now, I don't know how Ham will help—he's just like all of you. He has not yet developed any noticeable ability from the astral plane."* Misha kept a straight face though he was lying to the children.

"I can't wait to do more than just communicate telepathically. The only one from our group who has a special ability is Manchi. She's able to see energy in all matter," Magnus pointed out.

"Mag, don't worry. One day you'll have your ability and you—" Manchi answered mentally, and then stopped mid-sentence. *"Misha, we're not alone,"* she continued to say mentally, but in a way that only Misha could hear.

"Manchi, you okay?" one of the other girls asked, confused.

"Yes, Kyra, I'm all right."

Misha addressed all the kids, *"Class, I must do something with Manchi now. Please return to your huts."*

All the kids responded, "Okay," in unison and made their way to their huts.

"Who do you see?" Misha asked.

"There's a girl standing right in front of you," Manchi replied. *"She has long black hair and she's wearing a white gown. Her energy is a color I've never seen before."* Then she stiffened with fear. *"It's a scary chalk-white color."*

"It's not polite to talk about people, especially in front of them," the scary-looking girl said in an eerie voice and let out an evil laugh. She revealed herself to Misha, so he could see her standing before him.

"You should sleep," the young girl told Manchi mentally and waved her off with a flick of her wrist.

Manchi fell to the floor, seemingly asleep.

"Don't hurt her!" Misha said angrily.

"Don't worry, it's not her time yet. I'm here to play with *you*," the girl said, sneering at Misha.

"Wait! You were in my vision months ago," Misha remembered suddenly.

"Oh, how nice, you remember me," she said, laughing.

"You're Alma, right?" Misha asked.

She burst with laughter. "You're too funny. That's my

sister. My name is Corazon," she said, floating through the air a foot off the ground.

But Ham said Alma was the evil one, Misha thought to himself.

"Who is Ham?" Corazon asked.

Misha eyes grew wide as he realized the strange girl could read his private thoughts. He quickly meditated upon nothingness.

Corazon chuckled. "You're trying to block your thoughts." She squinted and focused harder on reading them.

"Stop it!" he yelled as a burst of energy emanated from his head and hit the girl.

Corazon was forced back two feet, and she laughed harder. "Oh, good! So you do want to play?" She gazed down at the ground. Soon, the dirt began swirling and clumped together to create two gnomes, with yellow eyes and sharp teeth. The three-foot tall men looked at Corazon, waiting for their command.

"Oh, you're hungry?" she asked them. She pointed to Misha and instructed, "You can eat him."

The gnomes turned to Misha and growled.

"Wait! Why are you doing this?" Misha asked her.

"Because I want to play!" Corazon snapped.

Slowly, the monstrous gnomes approached Misha in a menacing way. They leapt toward him. But before either could reach him, Misha lashed his hand at the dwarves and encased them in two clear bubbles. They began floating upwards, high in the sky until they could no longer be seen.

"You suck, Misha!" Corazon yelled. "I really liked them."

"Why do you do such things?" he asked.

Corazon giggled. "Because you won't."

"What do you mean?"

"You are the stupidest boy on the planet! You were chosen by IT to have limitless power and all you had to do was destroy a little city!" Corazon said, with an awkward twist of her head.

"But I guess we should thank you because if you weren't so useless, my sister and I wouldn't have our powers. Now, IT has chosen us for the task."

Misha narrowed his eyes. *"Why would you want to go along with something so horrible?"*

"Horrible?" Corazon burst with laughter. "You really are stupid!"

Misha subconsciously thought of Ham again. *But Ham agreed that it would be horrible… of course it would be.*

"WHO IS THIS HAM?" she yelled angrily.

Come on, focus, Misha, he said to himself.

"It doesn't matter, you're already doing IT's bidding without even knowing it," she told him.

"What is IT?" Misha asked.

The girl chuckled again.

"IT is what gave you life! IT is what gave us our abilities! IT has made you kill!" she answered, laughing.

"I have never killed in this lifetime!" Misha exclaimed. Then suddenly, he remembered he caused his parents' and grandparents' death.

Corazon circled him, sneering. "Since you didn't want to be the catalyst for IT's bidding, we will do it for you, and there's nothing you can do to stop us. IT will not repeat the same mistake twice so IT has granted us greater powers and greater knowledge of the overall purpose. And if you get in our way, we'll kill you painfully!" A burst of bright light crackled around her and she vanished.

Just then, Manchi began to wake and asked, "What happened?" She looked up and saw that Misha's energy was quite dull. "Misha, are you okay?" Manchi levitated from the ground.

He did not answer. Misha rose up off the ground and floated in the direction of the observatory alone as the sun set over the island.

Chapter 10

In New Orleans, nurse Hildred searched the halls of the hospital, looking for Brian. She spotted him at the far end of the hallway, talking to the parents of one of his patients.

"Thank you, doctor. We can see that Naweed is happier and doing better than he was a few months ago," Naweed's mother said.

"Yeah, all the kids seemed to be in brighter spirits lately," the psychologist told her.

Hildred approached them and said, "Doctor, I need to see you right away."

Brian turned back to the couple. "Will you excuse me please?"

"Sure, no problem," they answered.

"What's going on, Hildred?" Dr. Brian asked as they stepped away from the couple.

"It's John Doe— I mean, Jude," the nurse said.

"Is he okay?"

"Yes, well, actually… you know our protocol. Once we determine the identification of a John Doe, we input the information into the national database," Hildred started to say.

"Yeah, so?" Dr. Brian waited.

"Well, I entered it last night. This morning, I received a call from the local sheriff. He informed me that Jude has three warrants for his arrest in Newark, New Jersey. The police are on their way here to pick him up," she said nervously.

"Oh, no, that's terrible! Where is he now?"

"In the children's ward," she told him.

They both picked up the pace as they headed to the children's ward.

"What do we do?" Hildred asked.

"The police won't understand that Jude's not the same person who committed crimes in the past," Dr. Brian said regretfully.

"What if you're wrong, doctor? What if he's still the same?" Hildred asked. "You have too much confidence in someone you hardly know."

Dr. Brian gave her a hard look. "You've seen how he's been with the kids for months. He's made the kind of impact in their lives that doesn't come from a criminal. It's a positive impact that comes from a man with a good heart."

"But you yourself said he didn't know who he was until just yesterday," Hildred reminded him. "If he remembers now, then he knows he was a criminal."

They reached the doors of the children's ward and looked through the glass door. Kneeling before her, Jude was inside talking to Mabel.

"Hildred, I know you're a vegan." Dr. Brian said suddenly, catching her off guard. "Have you always been a vegan?"

"What?" She gave him a confused look, but answered anyway. "Uh… no, I turned vegan a couple of years back."

"Why did you become vegan?" he asked further.

"Well, a friend of mine who's a vegan took me to a slaughter house. After I saw how they treated animals, I swore I'd never be a part of hurting animals again," she explained, slightly irritated. She had told this story before.

"So you could say that all those years you ate meat were because you didn't know better?" Dr. Brian asked.

"Yeah, but—" Hildred tried to say.

"Well, it's the same for Jude. After spending time with the kids, and with me, and with some therapy, he's become aware of what he's done. Now he's able to make better choices about what to do with his life," Dr. Brian insisted.

"I don't know if that's the same, but I see what you're getting at," she responded. "So what do we do? The police said not to alert him that they're coming."

"I'll take care of Jude," Dr. Brian assured her. "You go to the reception area and stall the police when they get here."

"Stall them?" Hildred asked with a worried look on her face.

"I just need a little time with Jude before they take him," he said.

"Okay, Doc," she said, hesitantly.

Dr. Brian entered the large, colorful room where a dozen children were playing with toys. As usual, a few of them surrounded Jude.

"Uncle John, have you caught any bad guys lately?" Mabel asked him with big, bright eyes.

Naweed and Lillian stared at Jude, waiting for a response.

"Yes, Mabel, I caught two last night," Jude answered. "Now they're going to jail."

"Wow, that's so cool!" Naweed yelled out.

"You see! I told you so!" Mabel exclaimed. "He's the best policeman ever. Uncle John is my hero!"

Dr. Brian interrupted, "Children, I have to talk with John for a moment."

Naweed and Lillian stood up and walked towards the large television showing cartoons, but Mabel didn't move.

"Mabel, it's okay," Jude encouraged. "Go watch TV."

"But I want to stay here with you," she pleaded.

"I'll watch TV with you in a minute, I promise," Jude bargained.

"Okay, Uncle John, you promised." Mabel ran over to Naweed and Lillian.

"Hey, Doc, what's up?" Jude asked.

"Listen, Jude, this is a little hard for me to say—" Before he could finish what he planned to tell him, he noticed all the kids rushing towards the window.

Dr. Brian and Jude went over to the window with the kids and saw the flashing lights of a patrol car as it pulled up to the hospital.

Dr. Brian turned to Jude and could see the panic setting into him. "Look, Jude, that's what I was about to tell you… they're here for you."

Mabel overheard Dr. Brian. "Uncle John, do they need your help?"

At a loss for words, Jude looked at Brian.

"Yes, Mabel," Dr. Brian answered. "Uncle John is needed for an important case. He has to go help his friends."

"I knew it! I knew it! You see everyone!" Mabel yelled out. "My uncle John is going to go help the policemen." She ran up to Jude and gave him a big hug. "Please be careful, I love you."

Jude diverted his watery eyes so Dr. Brian couldn't see him. For the first time in all the years since his mother died, someone had told him she loved him.

"Okay, kids. Everyone say goodbye to Uncle John," Dr. Brian said. "He has to go now."

"Bye, Uncle John!" the children said.

Jude replied, "Bye, kids." He bent down and gave Mabel a kiss on the cheek.

Dr. Brian walked Jude towards the door. Jude looked back at the kids one last time. Mabel waved goodbye like a proud parent seeing her child off to school for the first day. Jude waved back.

Dr. Brian opened the door and, just as soon as he and Jude stepped out of the children's ward, they saw two police officers waiting. One officer moved in on Jude, grabbed him by the arm, shoved him around, and pushed him hard against the wall.

"No need to be so rough," Dr. Brian told them. "He's giving himself up."

"Mind your business, doctor, and step away!" the other officer demanded.

The officer attempted to cuff Jude until he noticed that he didn't have a right arm. He had no choice but to escort him by his only arm through the hospital.

Dr. Brian followed them through the hallways. "Hildred, go to the children's ward and make sure to keep the children away from the window."

Hildred nodded and rushed over to the children's room.

As they reached the police car, Dr. Brian said, "Remember, Jude, you are a different person than you were before. You are not the same man."

Just before being shoved inside the police car, Jude looked up at the children's ward windows. He was relieved to find the blinds closed.

"Dr. Brian, if you knew all the bad things I've done, you might not feel so confident about me being a changed man."

The officer put his hand on top of Jude's head and guided him roughly into his seat. Then the cop cuffed his left wrist to the metal grate between the front and the back of the squad car, and shut the door.

"Jude, you *are* a better man now!" the doctor yelled. "Have confidence in yourself!"

Jude stared back at him as the car pulled off. It flashed its lights as it left the hospital parking lot. Dr. Brian stood and watched until he could no longer see it anymore.

"You think we'll get any credit from Newark for picking this guy up?" the officer who was driving asked the other in the passenger seat. "His crimes aren't even in our state."

"Don't know, but it's good to get scum like this off the

streets," the other officer replied as he looked back and glared at Jude.

Jude waited and turned around to make sure the hospital was no longer in site. Then he looked forward again at the tree-lined road.

As the squad car continued along the road, Jude focused all of his attention on the handcuff, making it crystallize, and then shattering it to pieces. Quickly, Jude focused intently on the center of the car, doing the same to the metal chassis. Then the squad car split in half while still moving.

"What the hell?" one of the officers yelled in shock.

The front portion of the car continued down the road while the back part, where Jude was seated, slowed to a stop. The two cops watched in shock as Jude climbed out of the other half of the car.

"We need back up!" the driver yelled into his radio.

Both cops scrambled out of the front half of the car with their guns aimed at Jude.

Jude concentrated his thoughts on their guns and immediately crystallized them. Then he turned the guns to dust inside the cops' hands. The two officers yelled out in confusion. To humiliate them, Jude crystallized their clothes and turned them to dust, too.

Next, Jude focused on all of the carbon dust scattered on the street and re-formed it into a large diamond sphere. The sphere moved towards Jude, scooped him up and began to glide up high into the sky. Jude looked down at the two naked police officers as they scurried around trying to cover their bodies.

Gliding through the sky, Jude wondered where he would go and what he would do when he got there. Then he remembered the only person who not only accepted him unconditionally, but who worshipped him.

"I must go find my giant," he told himself.

Chapter 11

IN THE SWAMP LANDS DOWN the Mississippi River—a mile from the destroyed mansion—the largest man in the world walked towards a make-shift shelter. It was completely covered over by large brown tree leaves and held together by hardened mud. The giant man entered the shack and saw a small, attractive woman in her 30s, bent over a hot stove. She had light brown skin, an oval face, and dark wavy hair. The sweating woman wore jeans and a tattered white t-shirt, a large machete hanging from her belt, and a bone necklace on her neck.

"Sugah, what'cha wan fo supper?" the young Creole woman asked.

"Whatever you want, Savy," Montaña answered. "You know I will eat anything you make me."

The woman sniffed the air. "Smells like a downpour comin' any time soon. And yuh know how the gaters get then. It's best we eat the fish I caught this mornin'," Savy suggested.

"Okay," the giant agreed.

After dropping half a dozen fish into a deep pot of hot oil, she sprinkled a host of spices into the pot. "So, Sugah, tell me some more abou' ya friend who can fly," Savy prodded as she stirred the fish around in the oil.

"I… let my friend down." Montaña paused and lowered his eyes. "I made him a promise, but I did not keep it."

"Now, Sugah, if yuh story is true, then there was no heckuva way fo yuh to evah make it to New York City, the bad way he was. He would'a died on yuh," she tried to comfort him. "Yuh did the right thang by leavin' him at the hospital. Believe yuh me."

"I know, my Savy, but there is not a night that I do not think of him or where he is or if he is even alive." Montaña looked her square in the eyes and asked, "Did I really do the right thing?" Before she could answer, he stomped his foot down hard on the dirt floor and yelled, "I hate what I have done!"

The force of his pounding foot made some of the pots hanging on the wooden wall crash to the ground.

Savy bent down to pick them up and calmly said, "Now that wasn't very polite of yuh, was it, Sugah?"

"I am sorry, Savy. I just get angry at myself," he said. "I should have taken care of him."

"First time I laid eyes on yuh, I just knew yuh was a good man. A big manly man with a huge heart," she told him.

"Thank you, Savy," he said as he reached down and broke more wood for the fire.

"Just wish you weren't so hard on ya self," she added.

"One day, I will see him again. I just know it," the giant said.

"Ain't that a cheery thought," she said. "I hope so, too."

Savy pulled some of the crispy fried fish out of the pot. "I still don't get how he flew, but if yuh said he did, I believe it." She put the largest fish on a metal plate and handed it to Montaña.

Montaña picked up the plump fish with two fingers; it looked like a tiny guppy in his hand. Then he swallowed it down in one gulp. "Mmm, it is so good." He licked the tips of his fingers.

Savy took a bite of the smaller fish on her plate. "Yup, it's danged good."

"May I have another?" Montaña asked.

"Sure, Sugah." She passed him a thick fish. "Here ya go."

As the giant was about to eat the fish, he looked out the window at the gathering storm. The fish he was holding dropped onto his plate, he stood up from his chair and stepped out of the door of the wooden house.

"What's wrong?" Savy asked.

He looked up at the sky, and in the dark clouds, he saw an odd glimmer of light. Montaña's eyes opened wide. "Telaxtic! Telaxtic!" he yelled.

Montaña watched as a diamond sphere headed in his direction. The large sphere glided down into the swamp, near the giant.

Just then, Savy stepped out of the house and saw the diamond sphere floating down with a black man in jeans and a sweatshirt inside. "By my immortal soul, I can't believe my eyes," she said quietly.

As soon as the sphere landed, it melted to the ground.

Montaña immediately ran up to Jude and embraced him. "Oh, Master, I cannot believe it is really you," he said ecstatically. Then Montaña gasped when he saw Jude was missing an arm.

"Montaña, no need to call me Master or Telaxtic," he said. "I'm just Jude."

"Okay, Master— I mean Jude," Montaña said. "This is my friend Savannah Marie, but she likes to be called Savy." He turned to his right. "Savy, this is my mas— I mean, my friend, Jude."

"Pleased tuh make yuh acquaintance, sir," she said politely.

Jude half smiled. "Good to meet you, too."

"Come in," Montaña said, gesturing towards the shabby wooden house.

Jude entered and quickly scanned the inside of the modest home with his eyes.

Heading straight for the pots, Savy asked, "Would you like some suppah?"

"Sure," Jude answered.

Savy handed him a metal plate with a steaming hot fish on it.

Jude looked at Savy, waiting for her to pass him some utensils. Without saying a word, Montaña and Savy stared back at Jude. Finally figuring it out, Jude picked some fish off the bones with his fingers and popped it in his mouth. Montaña and Savy chuckled quietly.

"Montaña, I came to find you," Jude said in between bites.

"You plannin' on takin' my Manny?" Savy asked in a low voice.

Montaña sighed at the sight of sadness in her eyes. Savy had been looking out for him since the night of the explosion in the mansion. She had found him walking back from the hospital after he had dropped Jude off in the parking lot for the doctors to find. Savy was initially shocked by his massive frame, but the oddness wore off after a few weeks. She had made her home in the swamp bigger to accommodate him, and they had been living together for the past three months. Being a somewhat primal woman, Savy felt she had finally found a companion she could relate to. But now, their flying visitor had come to take him away.

"Do you want me to go with you?" Montaña asked Jude somberly. He looked to Savy, and then back at Jude.

It was obvious to Jude that Montaña had started making a home with Savy in the middle of nowhere, and appeared to be quite happy. Montaña seemed more confident and steady than before.

"I came because I wanted to thank you," Jude said humbly.

"If you hadn't taken me to that hospital, I would be dead so... thank you."

Montaña's lips trembled with happiness as he smiled. "So you didn't come to ask me to go with you?"

"No," Jude replied.

With a sigh of relief, Montaña asked, "What about the demons on the island?"

"Demons?" Savy asked.

"They're not demons," Jude corrected, "I was wrong about that, but I thank you for everything. I have to go now."

Montaña glanced down at Jude's right side, where his arm was missing.

Jude noticed, and he remembered the diamond arm he had made himself in the hypnotic dream. *I wonder if....* Then he stared hard at a pile of logs by the door until they crystallized, and then liquefied.

"What's happening?" Savy asked, shocked.

Montaña put his arm around her shoulder. "Do not worry, Savy."

Slowly, a thick strand of liquid diamond rose up and attached itself to his right shoulder. Jude focused carefully on the shimmering fluid extending from his shoulder, and it began to take shape of an arm and a hand. Jude flexed and extended his diamond right hand, which was as hard and solid as normal diamond when he wanted it to be, but still could be flexible.

Savy gasped in disbelief, and said once more, "By my immortal soul—"

"I always knew you were a god, Jude," Montaña said.

"Look, I gotta go," Jude said as he shook Montaña's hand. His large diamond hand was still tiny compared to the giant's hand. Smiling proudly, Montaña gave him a nod of the head. "Where are you going to?"

Jude walked out the door and looked back to find

Montaña and Savy holding hands. "I'm going to the island," he replied.

Jude created another diamond sphere and climbed into it. As it zipped away, Montaña and Savy waved him off.

Chapter 12

ALMA STOOD IN THE CENTER of her room, blinking from the burst of blinding light. A tall man with a pale, haggard face was standing inside the light. He wore a black trench coat specked with fresh blood. The man growled at the girl.

"I've done what you asked," the tall man said angrily. "I've killed the singer. Now fix me!"

"Plaaaaay niiiice, Fraaank Leeeeee," the young girl said in an eerie voice, then giggled.

A voice suddenly echoed from every direction of the room. "Corazon, maybe we should let him go."

Puzzled, Frank Lee's head jerked around, searching for where the voice had come from. Then he stopped and turned back to the little girl. Frank always felt that Alma, who his bosses—the twins—kept in hiding, was strange. And judging by all the information he had read on her, she had mysterious abilities that no one understood. But Frank had never read anything that suggested she might be violent in any of the files. Now, the young girl seemed to him like two different people.

"Alma, you always spoil my fun," the little girl said aloud.

Finding it hard to speak, Frank Lee growled, "Are you Alma or Corazon?"

The disembodied voice echoed once more, "We are sisters sharing one body."

"Don't tell him anything!" Corazon shouted.

Frank Lee realized that Alma's voice was the softer and kinder of the two, and Corazon's was the higher and more excited-sounding one.

"Alma, please convince your sister to let me go," he asked in a calm voice.

The girl said, "Corazon, why do we need him? Let's play with someone else."

She tightened her fists. "No. You are mine," she said, staring at Frank Lee.

Frank Lee felt overwhelming pressure in his head, and fell to his knees.

Corazon urged, "Alma, go to the island! Go play with them!"

"Yay, I'm gonna go play with them!" the voice agreed. "And I'll see my friend Lilly!" The echoing voice trailed off.

Still in agony, Frank Lee said, "Okay, what do you want me to do now?" He knew that he had to give in to the girl's requests until he figured out a way to escape and get his body back to normal.

"Youu muuust gooo tooo theee islaaand aaand kiiill eveeryooone," Corazon screeched, and then giggled. "GO!"

Bright light burst from Frank's body, and he disappeared suddenly. Frank Lee's body was catapulted through the air at lightning speed, and he knew he was headed for the island. Wincing from the constant pain that Corazon inflicted on him, Frank recalled his childhood.

Born into extreme poverty in Chengdu, China, Frank never knew his family. Crying inside a cage meant for a large dog was the earliest recollection he had. The cage was used to carry children sold into slavery. To stop the crying, his captors drugged him. Frank's most vivid childhood memory was of the day he was sold to one of the wealthiest men in China. He didn't know how much the stranger paid for him, but it was clear to young Frank that he belonged to the man.

For the better part of Frank's life, his meticulous owner taught him many things, including the art of stealth, discipline, assassination, and most importantly, a set of rules to follow. One of the rules was to never harm a child or a woman. Frank Lee had killed countless men in his professional career as an assassin, but he had never broken that rule.

Frank was aware of the island because he never stopped logging into the twin's computers for updates; he used a password that they were not aware of. So he knew that he was on his way to an island filled with young children, as well as Angelis. The code he had lived by his entire life was not negotiable, and every fiber of his being rebelled against the thought of breaking it.

Careening through the air, Frank thought, *I will kill myself on the island before I hurt a child or Angelis.* When the light began to dissipate and his vision cleared, he saw that he was not on the island at all, but still in the little girl's room.

"So you think you will not listen to me?" the irritated girl said through gritted teeth, standing before him.

Frank was speechless. He realized that she was testing him.

"You are still too human," she said, with shining, jet-black eyes.

Frank dropped to his knees and shouted out in pain. His cries quickly turned to beast-like howls. Frank's finger nails grew out like long talons and his face became elongated. His thin nose and his ears retreated into his face, leaving holes in their places. The wrinkled, colorless skin covering his body became scaly and the last of his hair fell out. Lastly, his eyes, which had been bloodshot but still human, turned as black as Corazon's.

The girl looked into his dark eyes and saw no hint of

humanity left. "Now you are ready, Frank Lee! Go kill them!" she said, smirking.

Light burst from him once more and the man-creature disappeared.

Chapter 13

A BRIGHT LIGHT BURST IN the sky above the rising sun. *I'm still not used to traveling at the speed of light,* Angelis thought as she floated above the sandy beach of the island. *It was just night time in Australia and here it's dawn.*

Angelis noticed that the light was on in Quintin's hut. Either he had gotten up super early or he had never gone to sleep, she assumed. *What a workaholic.* She turned her eyes to the roof of the hut she shared with Tenny and remembered Gemini's reassurances about their relationship. *I never thought I would be living with a boyfriend at the age of nineteen, but everything that's happened has made me feel older than I am. Gemini was right that some problems are inevitable, but I wouldn't trade my life for anything right now.*

She lowered herself to the ground, walked through the trees and entered her modest home. Tenny was sleeping curled up, hugging a pillow. Angelis carefully moved it aside and nestled herself into his arms.

Tenny woke up and caressed her hair. "I'm sorry for being such a jerk," he said.

Angelis shushed him. "It's okay," she said. "Go back to sleep."

In Quintin's hut, a black metal claw flexed its fingers on

the work table, seemingly on its own. It had four long talons and a hollow interior. *This glove should make Lilly Roonka happy,* Quintin thought. *She could scratch through anything and it will be able to grip better than her paws can.* He was a little concerned with Lilly Roonka's requests for more and more weapons, but he enjoyed the chance to explore different uses for his new metal. Quintin viewed the weapons as puzzles and tried not to think about how dangerous they actually were.

Ten different computer monitors displayed English language news feeds from around the world. Keeping on top of the news made Quintin feel less out of touch with the rest of the world. Suddenly, he noticed that they were all reporting the same thing. One report stated, "Breaking News: singer Gemini found murdered after Australian concert." The metal claw stopped moving as Quintin's mind abruptly shifted focus. "That can't be true," he told himself. *Who would murder someone who brought joy to so many people?* Even as he thought it, though, he knew that there were many precedents in history for such a thing.

Quintin turned to Nano. He had designed Nano to be plugged into an Ethernet cable. Two hours after it had begun downloading information, Nano had reconfigured its own structure to receive satellite signals and it was now making even faster progress on downloading the entire Internet database.

"Is Gemini dead?" Quintin asked the black orb.

It responded, "There has been a massive influx of data suggesting that Gemini is deceased."

"Any data suggesting that he's not?" Quintin asked, hopeful.

"The percentage of claims that he is alive is statistically average for cases in which a celebrity is murdered."

Quintin used his mind to call across the jungle to Tenny. *"Come to my cabin right now! And don't tell Angelis, just come quickly."*

In the observatory, Misha was scanning through the minds of thousands of people all over the world, searching for more possible stars. Then, like a sharp ache, he began to feel many threads of despair running through the collective psyche of the world. They grew stronger and broader as more and more people seemed to experience the same thing at the same time. Misha zeroed in on the mind of a teenage girl in Toronto, Canada, who seemed to be feeling it acutely.

Gemini can't be dead, the teenager thought. *I can't live in a world without his music. The world is a terrible place if someone so wonderful can be murdered.*

Misha felt her sadness as acutely as if he were feeling it himself, and then he realized that, in fact, he was. Gemini was one of the greatest successes of his star program. *Who would murder him? Why?*

Misha was mature beyond his eleven years, but once more he felt like the child who had accidentally killed his entire family. *Is this my fault? Am I a murderer yet again?*

Tenny was shocked by what he saw on the monitors as they repeated the same horrible proclamation over and over again.

"I can't be the one to tell Angelis," Tenny said.

He and Quintin jumped back as Misha suddenly appeared before them in Quintin's cabin. His melancholy expression told the two of them that he had heard about Gemini. Tenny reached out to comfort him, and was surprised when his hand went right through Misha's shoulder.

"I'm still in the observatory," said Misha. *"This is merely an astral projection of my body. I see that you have both learned of Gemini's murder. The three of you should come here as soon as possible."*

Quintin and Tenny walked to the hut where Angelis slept.

Tenny roused her by kissing her neck softly. "Baby, I can't tell you why right now, but you need to come with us to the observatory."

Her eyes widened, but she trustingly got out of bed, still wearing her clothes from the concert, and slipped on a pair of sandals. The three made a silent procession through the trees. Once they were at the observatory, Misha pulled Angelis aside. Quintin and Tenny watched as he locked eyes with her, and they knew he was having a conversation with her that they could not be privy to.

Angelis' eyes grew fearful and remained locked into Misha's for a few more seconds before she collapsed on the floor, crying inconsolably.

"When did you know?" she shouted at Tenny. "Are you happy? You were always jealous of him!"

Misha addressed all three of them. *"Do not place blame where it does not belong. I know the sorrow that you all must feel, but perhaps answers will help to heal the pain. I know of the one person who can provide those answers."* Misha pointed to the comatose body of Ham, lying on his pillow bed. *"We must enter his mind,"* Misha instructed.

Chapter 14

MISHA HELD TENNESSEE AND ANGELIS' hands. And Angelis' held Quintin's. *"I must concentrate very hard to enter the astral plane where Ham is,"* Misha said. *"Close your eyes and try to clear your minds to help me focus."* Of course, when someone tells you not to think, it's pretty much guaranteed to cause the opposite reaction, and Tennessee was embarrassed by the naked image of Angelis that popped into his head.

Then Tennessee sensed the world around him dissolving. Even with his eyes closed, he could feel the corporeal world becoming less real while his body felt lighter and lighter. There was a disorienting feeling of being jerked back and forth violently. The ground under his feet began to resolidify. *"Where's the sand? This isn't the desert."*

When he opened his eyes, Tennessee's face was flushed. *Did my previous thoughts somehow become visible?* But it was not Angelis he saw before him. It was Scarlett Johansson. Naked. And she was doing jumping jacks. Tennessee, Quintin and Angelis all looked at Misha in shock. Then Tenny and Quintin looked at Scarlett Johansson.

Angelis punched Tenny in the arm and asked, *"Where have you taken us, Misha?"*

"This is the astral plane that Ham is in," Misha responded.

"Hey, all we got was a desert?" Quintin asked, smiling. *"Thanks a lot, Misha!"*

"Ham," Misha mentally projected, *"Where are you?"*

A middle-aged man with salt-and-pepper hair appeared before them. *"Hello, Tennessee, my friend,"* he said. Then he introduced himself to Quintin and Angelis. *"Sorry about the setting, little lady,"* he told Angelis. *"I can't really control where I end up."*

"Where are we?" Quintin asked, *"Is that really Scarlett Johansson?"*

"No," Ham chuckled. *"We're in the dream of a sixteen year old boy. And believe me, this is mild compared to some of the others. I've seen some crazy stuff. I'll explain more about why I'm here later, but for now I'll just tell you that I'm in hiding from a very powerful being who wants to read my mind. In order to keep her from finding me, I've discovered a way to do what I call 'dream drifting.'*

"When the mind is in its deepest sleep, it emits only delta brain waves. These waves are very powerful, and tend to collect and run together in a sort of atmosphere of delta energy surrounding the earth. Most people are solidly tied into their own specific channel, but a few can occasionally dip into that massive reservoir of the delta waves, thus people having prophetic dreams or visions of others' lives.

"Sorry," he smiled, *"I'm blabbing on. Basically, I figured out a way to drift around in the atmosphere of delta waves, floating from dream to dream, never knowing where I'll end up. And if even I don't know where I'll end up, then it must be impossible for somebody else to know."* Then Ham added, *"it's certainly an interesting form of tourism. The human mind is much stranger than most people would imagine."* Though he half-smiled, there was a great deal of worry in his eyes.

Then, without warning, the group found themselves in

the middle of a screaming argument between a Chinese man and woman. The three teens didn't understand a word. After watching the dispute for a moment, Ham walked up to the couple and began speaking to them in Mandarin Chinese. When he was done speaking, the couple embraced and kissed passionately.

"They can see you in their dreams?" Quintin asked.

"Yes," Ham replied. *"I usually try not to interfere, but if someone is having a nightmare or if there's a clear way to improve someone's life, I do my best to help. This is the wife's dream and she thinks her husband is cheating on her. But he isn't. I told her so and that she should trust him when she wakes up."*

The couple disappeared, and the group found themselves at an office, watching a man intently working at a computer. *"I can always tell when people work too much,"* Ham said. *"It's all they dream about."*

"Wait, how did you know that the husband wasn't cheating?" Angelis asked.

Ham looked over at Misha. *"The power I gained from the desert was very important, but also very dangerous. Perhaps too powerful,"* Ham said. *"I developed the ability to know all things that have happened in the past and that are happening in the present, as well as their relative significance. But please understand, I am not all-knowing. I can't see the future, because the future is not yet written, but I can predict possible futures based upon patterns of the past.*

"I can't see all things at all times—that would drive me insane." Ham smiled wryly. *"I am able to ask a specific question in my head and learn the answer because I can see the connections between all things, the causes and effects, and I can rapidly put it all together. When I asked whether that husband was cheating on his wife, I saw a series of events prior to her suspicion, all of which lead to him being a faithful husband."*

Ham's cheerful smile disappeared. *"My newly acquired powers have allowed me to know many things, some of which perhaps should be shared with all of you."* He paused. *"There is a girl, Alma, who is in possession of a massively destructive force. She has the ability to absorb the powers of others, and has probably already gained all of yours, including yours, Misha. She does not know of me yet, but if she were to develop my powers, it could mean the end of the world. This is why I hide in dreams."*

Angelis, Tenny and Quintin were so enraptured by Ham's explanation that they barely noticed they were in the presence of a small boy playing an intense game of checkers with a Tyrannosaurus Rex. *"This boy is but one of the many I must protect by remaining in hiding, even if it means my death."*

"This Alma girl is such a great threat?" Angelis asked.

"Yes," Ham said, *"but she is not the origin of the problem. The entity that created her is the source of the danger. It is the same entity that created Misha."*

The three friends shared looks of surprise. Misha's origins had always been shrouded in mystery.

Ham continued, *"This entity has great power, and has no corporeal form as it would be understood in this universe. It was born before the birth of our universe. It came from a different dimension, one of two that collided about 13.76 billion years ago. This collision brought about the event commonly known as the Big Bang."*

Quintin stared at Ham incredulously and said, *"The precise cause of the Big Bang is one of the greatest mysteries of modern science. And you claim to know it?"*

Ham looked at him solemnly. *"Quintin, I can tell you exactly how the universe was created, but my mental energy would be better spent contemplating matters that will directly affect us."*

"Please tell me," Quintin begged. *"I need to know!"*

Ham had empathy for such burning curiosity. It had plagued him before he was cursed with omniscience. *"When the two dimensions collided,"* Ham explained, *"they created a super-concentrated ball of matter. Energy fused from both dimensions and, although most beings from both dimensions perished, there were a few strong and resilient ones who survived. The entity that created Misha and Alma was one of them. Sometimes, we humans see these few survivors as gods. They were highly evolved beings in their own dimensions, allowing them to survive the catastrophe of the collision, and they were more powerful than the native beings of this universe. These 'gods' roamed the newly forged universe, experimenting to rid themselves of loneliness. Some were mortal, but others may not be."*

The group was listening raptly. Ham continued, *"The entity in question requires an input of energy in order to live, just like us. Every time we eat a vegetable or an animal, we are gaining energy from breaking it down. One must destroy something in order to gain its energy. For eons, the entity in question gathered energy from stars, creating asteroids to bash into them and release their trapped energy. Then it created an asteroid to smash into Earth for no other purpose than to get a rush from the release of freed energy. But what it did not realize is that a different kind of life form had started its own little experiment here. That asteroid is what killed the dinosaurs, and the sudden release of the energy of sentient beings was intoxicating. It had found a new hunting ground. When human beings eventually evolved, it discovered that the most satiating food was the life-force of these new animals.*

"The human body and mind require immense and complicated forms of energy, and the release of this energy is quite powerful. The being I speak of has a different relationship with time than we do. It only needs to feed about once every two-thousand years. And when the hunger rises, he gorges on human life-force by bringing about a massive calamity. Since the entity does not have a physical form, it creates a conduit in order to help gather the energy it needs. For stars and uninhabited planets, asteroids were sufficient, but gathering the energy found in humans is much more difficult. Misha has been its energy gatherer in this regard. This lifetime would make it the twelfth occasion that Misha has done this for it, if Misha were to perform his assigned task.

"*This entity allows Misha to unlock the potential of the human mind. He could have made a being who would cause direct disasters, but he believed that the more complex the devastation was, the more energy could be released and the more satiating the meal. Misha was programmed to find a mentally receptive individual, who he could give specific abilities to. That human would gain the ability to create monsters whose sole purpose was to destroy. In the past twelve cycles of this process, the entity has killed thousands of people, and entire civilizations to feed itself by using Misha. His hunger grows greater each time.*

"*This time, Misha unconsciously chose Tennessee as the monster-maker. But for some reason, Misha—for the first time ever—deviated from his programming and developed a conscience. Personally, I believe this happened because every human consciousness has a natural tendency towards empathy, and when given enough time, will develop it fully.*

"*So the entity created a new conduit, Alma. And having learned of this human tendency for empathy, he created within her a fail-safe alter-ego that lacked humanity. This alter-ego, Corazon, is the evil one. Alma is just her hostess and power gatherer.*"

Ham paused for a moment to give the others a moment to take in all he'd said. Tenny, Angelis, Quintin, and even Misha, were so riveted by all the information, they hadn't even noticed the series of bizarre dreams they were floating through.

Then suddenly and at once, all four of them realized that they were smack in the middle of a horrendous scene of hell, straight out of *Dante's Inferno*.

"*The dream of a guilty Catholic,*" Ham told them, smiling at the simplicity of such visions of the universe. He walked up to a pained man chained to a pyre as he was being burned alive and said, "*I am a messenger from God. He wants me to tell you that you are a good person and that you will be going to heaven.*"

"*Wait!*" Quintin said when Ham returned to the group. "*Are you saying that heaven and hell are real?*"

"*No,*" Ham responded. "*The truth is much more complicated. But part of being omniscient is that I know exactly what to say in order to bring about the best result. This is a good man and he'll lead a much happier life from now on.*"

The hellish scene disappeared, and the group found themselves in a swamp, filled with a menacing pairs of pliers the size of alligators. "*Just ignore the dreams,*" Ham told them, "*there's too much to talk about.*"

Tenny tried his best to ignore the giant, snapping pliers. "*I want to know something, Mr. All-Knowing. What does Helaxtic, Telextic, Chronos, Sing mean? When we first met Misha, those words were written on a black stone, but Misha said he had never written them. It's been bothering me ever since. Where did those words come from and what do they mean?*"

Ham said, "*Alma wrote those words. They're her names for you three and Jude, and they have very interesting meanings.*"

Just then the group found themselves in a new dream. At first, the young people ignored it as instructed by Ham. It didn't appear to be a very interesting dream anyway—just a little girl playing with dolls. Then they noticed the look of horror on Ham's face.

"*Ah! So you're the famous Ham,*" said the ashen, black-eyed girl. She walked toward him and her walking doll followed her. "*What goodies do you have for me?*"

Ham could not believe that of all the dreams in the world, he would have the horrible luck of ending up in Alma's dream. She must have managed to draw him to her. And he could already sense her probing into his mind. But Ham had prepared for just such an emergency. He had taught himself to control his bodily functions and could stop his heart in an instant. Before doing so, Ham projected an image of a luxurious penthouse apartment in New York City into Misha's mind. Next, he transferred his own mind-energy into a trusty receptacle. These last tasks done, he turned off his heart as easily as if it was a light switch.

Dead, Ham fell to the ground, and Tenny, Misha, Quintin and Angelis stood slack-jawed, in shock. Immediately after, they were all whisked back to Misha's observatory, as Ham no longer had an astral plane in which to dwell.

Angelis was the first to recover from the shock. "What the fuck do we do now?"

After a long pause caused by the added shock of hearing Angelis' cursing, Misha said, *"I think we have to go to New York City."*

Chapter 15

THE THREE FRIENDS STOOD STILL, staring at the solid walls of the observatory. Though the rapidly changing dreamscapes had ceased, their current surroundings seemed no more real. Misha floated in the midst of them with his eyes screwed shut, tears streaming from the corners.

Ham lay on the same pillow bed as before. Misha floated over to him, placed his hands on Ham's heart, and declared, "*He's dead.*

"*Before he took his own life, he showed me the location of the child, Alma. She resides in a penthouse in New York City. That is why we must go there. But the matter is rather complicated.*"

"Why?" Tenny asked. "Obviously, we simply need to go to New York and kill this Alma girl."

Quintin interjected, "It's not that simple. If she has all of our powers, like Ham said, and possibly more powers that she's gotten from other sources, how can we defeat her?"

"Right," agreed Angelis. "And do you really believe you can kill a little girl, even if you know she's evil? Besides, I'm not sure what Ham meant, but he said Alma wasn't completely evil."

Misha gave them a grave look. "*When I was still a small child, I vowed to never take another life after accidentally killing my family. My voice put them in astral planes that caused their lives to seep away. I took a vow of silence, and I will not kill anyone, no matter how evil they are. Perhaps it's selfish, but I would rather lose the battle than win it by killing."*

While Misha was the youngest of the four, Angelis, Quintin and Tenny looked to him as their leader. If he said they couldn't kill, then they would need to find another way.

"What if we trap her somehow?" Angelis suggested.

"That would be harder than killing her," countered Quintin. *"If we were to trap her, we'd never manage to keep her there."*

All three debated various possibilities when Quintin interjected, *"I may have another resource that we can consult. Come with me."*

Quintin led Tenny and Angelis to his hut, while Misha stayed behind in the observatory. Angelis was the only one who had not known about Nano. He introduced the black sphere and explained all of its capabilities and its current project. "Nano, how much information have you downloaded from the Internet?"

"Currently, I have assimilated 62% of all available information," Nano replied in a humming voice.

"Have you, by any chance, gotten to any tactical military plans or super-weapon diagrams?"

"No," Nano answered. "Military information appears to be heavily guarded. It will take a day or two to break through."

"Okay, Nano," Quintin said. "Sift through all the information you've gathered so far and let me know how someone could defeat an opponent of equal power."

Nano hummed. "I have come up with a relevant piece of information. When two objects have the same mass and density, speed becomes the deciding factor in which an object can cause more damage to a third, unequal object."

"Okay…" Tenny said doubtfully. "So you're saying that we need to move fast, but we still need to know *how* we move and how to work together to combine our powers."

Nano responded, "A complex machine can accomplish things that the individual parts, separately, cannot. The parts must interact with each other perfectly in order for the machine to function."

Tenny rolled his eyes. "Your computer's very helpful, Quintin," he said sarcastically.

"Hey," defended Quintin. "We're not giving Nano enough information to work with. If we could give it our precise powers and limitations, Alma's precise powers and limitations, diagrams of the relevant environments and any possible variables, it could give us a perfect plan!"

Tenny stared at him. "Like I said, veeery helpful."

Suddenly the sphere began to vibrate violently and seemed to growl.

"Tenny! You offended Nano!" Angelis scolded.

"Um, I don't think it's capable of being offended," Quintin said. "Something else must be going on."

"I believe I am being invaded by an unknown virus," Nano stated, as it continued to shake violently. "Activating all known anti-virus programs."

Quintin was disturbed. "This is not supposed to happen! Nano is the most advanced computer ever! Who could create a virus capable of infecting it?"

Tenny, Angelis and Misha looked on nervously. If it was Alma, she would now know everything that Nano knew, and the group would lose their only advantage.

Then the group heard a familiar voice emerge from the sphere. "Nano is correct. You must work together seamlessly. But the machine that you're a part of is missing one of its key components."

They were all flabbergasted.

"Ham, is that you?" Angelis asked.

"Yes, it's me," Ham spoke from the black sphere. "I'm sorry I didn't tell you guys about this contingency plan, but I needed Alma to think I killed myself. The mind is merely a system of electronic data storage and assimilation, like a computer. I basically remotely uploaded myself into Nano, the only computer on Earth advanced enough to house me."

They all smiled, relieved. Quintin crossed his arms in front of him with pride in his creation.

Then Nano said, "Approval needed for new program."

"Program approved," Quintin responded. "File name is Ham. Allow access."

Nano buzzed and Ham's voice came through again. "I can help you formulate a plan, but it will be much more difficult to defeat her without killing her. You need the missing part of your machine."

Chapter 16

Manchi strolled around the hydroponic vegetable garden in the dimming evening light. Quintin had developed the garden by using innovative agricultural techniques to provide food for the residents of the island. But with all his technical prowess, he couldn't compare to Manchi and her ability of making things grow. She loved to wander through the plants, feeling their energy and sharing hers' with them. Because of Manchi, the fruits and vegetables on the island could easily have won top prize in any state fair.

Manchi stopped before a small tomato that was having difficulty thriving. The other tomatoes on the vine were robust and healthy, but they were robbing the small tomato at the bottom of its nutrients. Manchi cupped the tiny tomato with her hand and redirected the energy flow of the vine so it would provide more energy for the little tomato. Manchi always helped the underdog.

As a child growing up in Hong Kong, Manchi's mother had told her that the secret to making plants grow big and strong was to talk to them.

If only you knew, Mom, she thought.

A sudden burst of hostile energy disrupted Manchi. She focused on the intruder, and was confused by what she sensed.

His aura was gray, the sign of a conflicted soul. Splotches of white light burst through the swirling, dark grayness, like a gathering storm. She sensed that a moral war was occurring inside the man.

Stranger still was the burning red emanation surrounding the swirling grayness of his aura; it encircled him and trailed behind him.

Who are you?" Manchi asked telepathically.

He opened his mouth weakly, but all that came out was more of the red, fire-like energy. It frightened Manchi to near paralysis. Then the man lunged at her with a sharp object. She felt the cold steel pierce her stomach. For a quick second, Manchi wondered if the object was created with the intention of puncturing an eight-year-old's intestines. Then she dropped to the ground. As Manchi collapsed, she sent a desperate plea of help to Lilly Roonka, who was the only one left on the island, and who acted as its guardian.

Another being suddenly revealed itself before Manchi, but she knew that it was not Lilly Roonka. The aura of this second was muddled, but Manchi attributed this to her injured state.

Jude had come to the island in an attempt to understand what had happened in his recent past, and was extremely disturbed to find a haggard monster attacking the young child, Manchi. He thought back to the children he had connected with in the hospital and reacted immediately. Jude's visceral rage propelled his crystalline diamond daggers towards the attacker. The monster spouted blood from all parts of its body.

Seemingly unaffected by his injuries, it turned to Jude and threw a bayonet at him with great speed. But Jude blocked the blade with a rapidly created diamond shield. Once the monster realized defeat, he vanished, leaving behind pools of blood in the garden, and a fading red glow.

Jude knelt next to Manchi and cradled her head in his

hands. All he could think of were the terminally ill children left behind in the hospital, specifically Mabel. She had made him believe that he could be a good person. Jude couldn't save Mabel, but here was his opportunity to save another young girl.

"What was that?" Jude asked her.

Then suddenly Lilly Roonka leapt out from behind a tall squash vine, baring black talons. She had been in Quintin's cabin testing her new weapons when she heard Manchi's calls of distress. When she spotted Jude kneeling over Manchi's bloody body, she lunged at him with all the fury and anguish she'd built up after Jude's attack months before.

"Fucking rabbit!" Jude yelled and quickly made a thick diamond shield in front of himself and Manchi. He also recreated the diamond arm and attached it to his shoulder. Jude then leaned over Manchi and held the arm over himself and her reclining body.

Lilly Roonka shrieked, "You monster! I knew you'd come back! But I'm ready!" She laughed and pulled a spiked disc from the belt around her waist. Then she threw it at Jude with shocking precision. All those hours she'd spent practicing in the jungle were not in vain.

Jude's diamond shield shattered like glass, and the disc hit Jude's diamond arm, which was positioned over Manchi's head, and swerved slightly off course. The disc grazed Jude's cheek instead of splitting his head in two.

Oh, Shit! Jude thought. *What the fuck was that?* His diamond arm was broken in two. He congealed a diamond wall, four-feet thick, in front of him and Manchi, hoping it would protect them from Lilly Roonka's strange new weapon.

Lilly Roonka threw another disc, but this one only went halfway through the thicker diamond shield. Jude breathed a sigh of relief. Then Lilly Roonka lunged towards Jude's wall with her new glove. She tore at the diamond wall viciously, rapidly eating away at it. Shards of diamond fell around her as she grew closer to Jude. Just as she broke through, Jude reformed the shards of diamond into a ball, and thrust it at Lilly Roonka with all of his mental strength. It struck her in the stomach and sent her flying twelve feet.

She was dazed, but managed to get back up. "You horrible, horrible man!" Lilly Roonka yelled. "You killed the guardians, my friends! You hurt my Angelis! You need to die!" She threw two more spiked discs, but her aim was off and she missed Jude. One landed dangerously close to Manchi. This infuriated Jude.

Jude encased Lilly Roonka in a diamond orb and sent it hurtling through the air. He could see her clawing at its insides as it flew high above him. Off in the far distance, he thought he saw her escape from the orb and fall out of it.

"She just wanted to protect me." Jude heard in his mind.

"Are you ok?" he asked Manchi.

Suddenly, he saw Manchi's wounds begin to heal in front of him.

"I can direct energy," she said. *"The others believe I can only do it for plants, but I can do it for people, too."* Manchi then reached for Jude's bleeding face and held it. Soon after, he felt his wound close; it was surprisingly painful.

"I'm sorry," Manchi told him. *"My power is drained. You may have a scar."* Then she looked at him with gleaming young eyes. *"You're Jude, right? You're Tennessee's brother. Your auras are so similar. And you both have beautiful auras."* She fixed her gaze even more firmly on his. *"Everyone knows that matter can be transformed into energy, like fire, but what people don't realize is that energy can be transformed into matter, too."* Her gaze drifted away. *"I don't know why, but I felt like you might need to know that."*

Jude was a little uncomfortable with all her talk of auras and energy flow, so he asked, *"Where is my brother?"*

"He's in the city with the rest of them. New York City. They're

fighting an evil little girl who wants to destroy the city. You should go help them."

Both of them heard the rustling sound of a giant rabbit rushing through the jungle.

"I'm so tired," Jude said. *"I traveled all day to come here, then had to fight. And now I have to fly all the way to New York City to fight some little girl?"*

Manchi laughed. *"I can get you to New York at the speed of light. I taught the others how to do it, and now I'll teach you. I can direct the energy of all things and turn your energy into a beam of light. You'll learn how on your own once you feel how it works."*

Just then they heard Lilly Roonka grow closer.

"Don't worry, she's my friend," Manchi told Jude. *"She won't hurt me. Oh, and the little girl, she's not really a little girl."*

Before he could ask what she meant, Jude felt his corporeal being begin to dissolve. His body appeared to be turning to light. He felt free of the burden of who he was. Jude was intoxicated by the strong sensation of happiness. It was then that Lilly Roonka burst into the scene. She lunged at Jude as he felt himself evaporate. Jude watched her fall to the ground as though through a haze. Then all was white.

Chapter 17

In a burst of brilliant light, four people materialized in a penthouse in New York City, just across from the Empire State Building. For a brief moment they were taken aback by the lavish apartment—its luxurious décor and stunning view. Then they quickly focused their attention on the small girl in the center of the room. She was wearing pink pajamas and sat crossed legged with her back to the group.

"I'm sorry, Sangon, I didn't know she was going to do that," the girl said remorsefully.

The four people stepped around to see what the young girl was doing. Black stones were scattered on the floor in front of her with a word carved on each: Sangon, Manchi, Helaxtic, Telaxtic, Cronos, Sing and Misha.

The stone with the word "Sangon" was broken in half. The little girl picked up the two pieces and placed them together as if to see whether or not they would stick, but they fell apart when she let go. The stone that read "Manchi" was cracked, but slowly reconstructed itself before everyone's eyes.

"She can't be the monster that Ham spoke about," Angelis said to the others.

"Have you come to play with me?" Alma asked, without looking at them.

"No, Alma, we've come to stop you," Quintin said, trying to sound confident.

Alma levitated off the ground and glared at them. "Stop me? Stop me from what?"

Although the group believed Ham that the girl posed an imminent danger to them, her innocent demeanor made it difficult for them to apprehend her.

"Maybe she doesn't know," Tenny told the group. "Remember that Ham said it wasn't actually Alma, but her alter-ego Corazon that was the evil one."

At hearing the name Corazon, the girl's eyes turned jet-black, her skin became ashen, and she tilted her head to the side. "Where is Ham!? I don't believe that he's dead!" Corazon screeched like a banshee. "I don't like it when people keep secrets from me!" Corazon stopped and seemingly looked them all in the eyes at the same time. "Ham had the power of omniscience. How delightful. I see from your thoughts that this machine called Nano now contains him. That wasn't so hard to figure out. I'll just use Nano's powers for myself then."

Not knowing what else to do, Quintin created a sphere of Quintium around Corazon. She parted it like it was a beaded curtain and stepped out.

"I can manipulate matter as well as you, you idiot. The only reason I don't kill all of you now is because I need to make sure that I know everything you know. Unfortunately, I can't read the minds of dead people, as I've discovered. I'll soon have Ham's power of omniscience, and then I'll have no use for you." She closed her eyes, and then opened them looking frustrated.

"What? You can't absorb the powers of a machine?" Quintin taunted. "And don't even try stealing Nano. He won't respond to you."

Corazon knew that this was true after reading Quintin's

mind and learning that he had programmed Nano not to respond to anyone else.

"Ah!" Corazon said. "But if I have *your* abilities, I can reprogram it…"

Knowing that this was true, Angelis quickly produced a sensation of blinding whiteness around Corazon, Tennessee turned her pajamas into a mass of snapping snakes, and Quintin ensconced her in another orb of Quintium. All three teens then concentrated their energy on shooting the orb through the penthouse roof and out into space.

"By the time she sorts through it all and frees herself, the lack of oxygen should kill her," Quintin said tentatively.

"*I said, no killing,*" Misha insisted.

Up until then, the three teens had forgotten Misha, who had quietly observed them.

"*I'm sorry, Misha,*" they all responded.

"*But she was going to reprogram Nano,*" Quintin explained. "*And she has all our abilities, including yours, just like Ham told us.*"

"No need to cry, you little fool," Corazon said from her canopy bed, where she lay back comfortably. "If you think your silly trick could kill me, then maybe I *do* know everything you sorry bunch of weaklings know. Let me say it slowly so you can understand: you. can't. hurt. me. I am the embodiment of a being that has existed since before your planet or galaxy or universe ever existed. You cannot destroy me. I am everlasting."

The group looked at each other with panic. They had thought that not killing Alma or Corazon was their choice; that it was an act of mercy. But it had never occurred to them that it could be literally impossible.

"Time for it to feed now," Corazon announced. "I'll keep you guys alive so you can see how powerless you really are."

As she raised her thin, pale arms, the entire top of the damaged penthouse roof broke off in pieces, which floated away into the sky like helium balloons. The teens imagined what the people on the streets below and those on the Empire State Building observation deck across the street must be thinking, first seeing the Quintium sphere and now the floating roof pieces.

The pieces began to clump together, along with blobs of Quintium and a few unlucky pigeons. The mixture began to take on a conical shape.

"Not enough matter!" Corazon complained.

The group then saw taxis flying up off of the ground, with drivers and passengers still inside, and they mixed in with the forming mass.

"Those are people!" Angelis shouted at Corazon. "You're killing them!"

Corazon laughed in a high-pitched tone. "It's all just matter."

A massive pyramid was forming in the sky. Corazon began decorating it by pulling Gargoyles off of nearby buildings and sticking them on the pyramid. "Wonderful!" she said. "But it's missing something."

After a moment, the guardrail of the Empire State Building observation deck broke off from the building. People leaning against it to get a view of the destruction fell to their deaths. Some managed to clutch onto the rail and hung on for dear life. Corazon simply placed the guardrail atop the pyramid like a crown. Those who were hanging onto it turned into stone.

As Corazon admired her handiwork, panels opened on all four sides of the pyramid and dozens of purple demons, twelve-feet long and with large wingspans, flew out in all directions.

The dragon-like demons landed on surrounding buildings, ripping through walls and eating people inside the exposed rooms. One ate an entire news helicopter that had arrived to cover the event.

Quintin tried to encapsulate some of the demons in

Quintium spheres, but they clawed right through them. Then he caught sight of their black talons. "Oh no," he said.

Corazon had created the demons with Quintium talons.

Another burst of light flashed in the penthouse, and Jude suddenly appeared near Corazon.

"What the hell? You're supposed to be dead!" Tennessee yelled. He saw that Jude's right arm was made of a smooth, clear material.

Groggy, Jude asked, "Where am I?"

"Can things get any worse?" Angelis asked. "We can't fight Jude and all these demons and this crazy little bitch all at the same time!"

"Hello, Telaxtic," Corazon said without looking, as she released more and more demons from her airborne pyramid.

The group stood back waiting for Jude to attack. But to their disbelief, he simply watched them, confused.

"What the hell is going on here!?" Jude shouted. "Actually, what's going on in the entire fucking world lately?"

"I don't know how you got here, Jude, but if you want another battle, I'm ready," Tennessee said. He turned the bureau in the room into an eight-foot-tall, dark gray, hulking creature that resembled a dolphin on steroids. With fangs.

The creature leapt onto Jude, grabbing him by the neck, and threw him against a wall. For a second, Tennessee wondered why Jude had not attacked them. He couldn't understand why Jude wasn't fighting back.

Jude transformed his body into a malleable diamond substance. No matter how viciously the creature attacked him, Jude seemed to feel no pain.

"A fucking vampire dolphin?" Jude said, laughing. "You're one weird dude, Tenny. But anyway, I'm not here to fight you guys. I'm not sure how I feel about any of you. I just know I didn't come to fight you. I mean, look around. I'm not the threat here."

Tenny turned to see Quintin and Angelis desperately

trying to kill the flying demons faster than new ones were being created. Misha sat looking shell-shocked in a corner and rocking back and forth. Tenny knew it was a losing battle. He shrugged and directed his gray creature towards one of the demons. Tenny's strange creation was soon eaten whole.

"That little Asian girl told me about this evil kid," Jude said from the mouth of his diamond body. "I don't get why y'all can't beat a little girl on your own."

He focused on all the flying demons he could see, turned them into diamonds, and then reduced them to carbon dust before they hit the ground. The ash swirled down , coating the buildings and streets below in black. A stray demon flew over to see what had happened to its siblings; it was rapidly reduced to black powder.

"There. Was that so hard?" Jude asked, smirking. "Now I'll take care of this teeny, weeny little girl you guys are so scared of."

Corazon smirked back at Jude. Then the monster Jude had seen back in the island garden leapt onto his back and stabbed him in the shoulder.

Why does this hurt? I'm a diamond, Jude thought. Then he realized that he had somehow been changed back to flesh and blood. And he was missing an arm again.

"Corazon has all our powers," Tenny told Jude frantically, "Don't even try to fight her; she just learns from it. We don't know what to do."

"Good advice," she said. "That was very naughty, Jude! Now I have to make all new demons!" Corazon raised her arms dramatically and began waving them like an orchestra conductor. As she hummed the *1812 Overture*, new monsters flew out of the pyramid, each larger and uglier than the last. "Da da da da da da DUM DUM DUM!" she sang.

"You know, they originally performed this song with cannons," Corazon informed no one in particular. "What a good idea!" A cannon appeared beside her. "Da da da da da da" BOOM! The cannon fired loudly. The cannon ball hit one of the new demons, which fell about a hundred stories and exploded upon impact. The area surrounding the site was now covered in orange goo on top of the carbon dust. "Oops," said Corazon, giggling.

Her manic giggle became more and more high-pitched until suddenly it turned into a wracking cough. After she caught her breath, the girl's eyes had turned brown again and a pink color was apparent in her skin. Alma quickly healed Jude's shoulder wound and, to his amazement, when she touched the shoulder missing an arm, his real, flesh-and-blood arm began to grow back.

Alma then changed the grotesque creature back into Frank Lee, who fell to the floor unconscious. Next, she picked up and held the stone that read "Sing" tightly in her hand and told Tenny and Jude, "Kill me before it's too late!"

But it already was. The black eyes and ashen skin were back, and the "Sing" stone fell from her hand. It vibrated when it hit the floor, but no one noticed.

Frank Lee slowly became aware of pain. His body felt like it had gone through a washing machine filled with rocks. He felt like himself again, though. His acute senses then came back in full. He knew that a battle was raging around him, and who its participants were. He kept his eyes closed, though, and remained absolutely motionless.

He knew that he would have only one chance to act. Alma was a child, and a female, and it went against everything he had ever believed to harm her, but he knew that if he could stop her, he would save many, many more women and children. He opened one of his eyes just the tiniest slit.

Directly next to his left hand was a jagged piece of metal, probably from one of the ultra-modern metal furniture pieces that the twins favored. Frank was right handed, but his left would have to serve. As quickly as a snapped elastic band, he gripped the metal, swung his arm around, and sent it flying towards Corazon's head. If it hit the right spot, she would die instantly.

His injuries and lack of skill with his left hand must have thrown off his aim, though. The metal grazed the top of her head, cutting it, but did not even render her unconscious. She became completely still, just for a second. Then she slowly spun around, her black eyes blazing as blood dripped down her face.

"You. Cut. Me," she stated, her voice like rusted iron. Frank Lee felt his body lift off the ground. Corazon pinned him into the air above her head. "I don't like you very much," she said. "You're not even fun, like these other morons. You need to learn what pain means."

As Corazon focused on Frank Lee, Angelis felt a sudden surge of power. Time seemed to slow down. *Where is this power coming from?* She wondered. Angelis had no way of knowing that before Alma had changed back into Corazon, she had imbued Angelis with the ability to absorb energy; it came from all around her, from the people screaming, from the demons flapping their wings, even from the stones in the buildings. As the world around her grew slower and quieter, she felt connected to all things. Angelis lifted an arm above her head and swung it around. She felt that simple motion reverberate across the universe.

Angelis had always believed that her power was next to useless, just altering color. She hadn't appreciated the fact that color was light not trapped by matter. She had been unnecessarily limiting herself. Quintin had power over matter, but she had power over everything that escaped matter. She already knew how to make herself and others travel at the speed of light, but she could see a way to travel faster than that.

Angelis knew that she had to stay a step ahead of Corazon, and told Tenny, Quintin, Misha, and even Jude, *"There's no time to explain, but I can send her back in time. Corazon just needs to have very specific qualities relating to color."* Then Angelis turned to Jude. "*She needs be a diamond, because diamonds reject all colors.*"

Quintin interjected, "*Hey, I can make a diamond as well or better than Jude can! His powers are nothing compared to mine!*"

Angelis ignored him, "*I don't know if I could do it with a diamond the size of her body, though. It would have to be smaller.*"

"*So we'll just compress it,*" Quintin suggested.

"*No, no, no, no, no!*" Misha repeated. "*That would kill her. No killing.*"

Jude briefly wondered why everyone was listening to this little kid who wasn't even helping in the fight. Then he remembered what Manchi had told him in the garden. He interrupted, saying, "*I think that I could turn her energy, her electrical essence, into a diamond. It would be very small and would also preserve her life-force.*"

Quintin stared down Jude. "*There's no way you can do that. If you could do that, then I could, too!*"

Corazon finally tired of torturing Frank Lee. The hatred that she felt for him was intense, and she wanted to vent it for longer, but she knew that she had a job to do. With a flick of her wrist, she sent him flying through the window. As he fell towards the broken street, he yelled out an old Chinese curse, directed at no one in particular.

"*This is no time to argue!*" Angelis scolded frantically. "*Any second she'll figure out what we're up to. Just do it, Jude!*"

Jude turned toward the tiny girl, who stood at the large window staring down. He began to pull the electrical impulses from her mind in thin diamond strands, flowing from her head like shimmering spider webs.

"What? No! What's going on? You can't do this! You don't have the ability!" Her voice grew quieter as more and more strands coalesced into a tiny diamond. Corazon and Alma's body fell to the ground, lifeless. The small diamond that contained every thought and memory that Alma and Corazon had ever had spun in the air.

Jude watched all the chaos outside. "Maybe when she's not here, it will all stop," he said aloud.

He continued concentrating on the spinning diamond, hardening it, smoothing its edges and making it beautiful, compressing the girl's energy into tighter and tighter molecules. Jude did not consider how much of one's own energy it took to turn another's energy into matter. Misha and the teens stared out at the destruction in the city and didn't notice the diamond threads crawling out of Jude's head as he focused on Corazon. Another, rough diamond was forming next to Corazon's. Angelis saw and knew what it might mean, but was busy concentrating on sending the Corazon diamond as far back in time as she could.

Suddenly, the room turned black. When the light returned, both Jude and the diamond had disappeared from sight.

"What happened to Jude?" Tenny asked with concern in his voice.

"I don't know," Angelis said. "Maybe the concentration was too much for him. Maybe he went with her…"

They turned to the nearest window. The swirling demons were turning to dust. Some still-living people fell out of them, only to die when they hit the pavement below. The pyramid went next, raining ashes down upon everyone in the penthouse. A single black stone was among the ashes. It stated "Soul."

The four walked over to the dead body of Corazon, which they saw was now the dead body of Alma. *"Poor girl,"* Misha said. *"She never asked for any of this. Any more than I did."*

He picked up the "Soul" stone and, without knowing why, placed it on top of Alma's chest, crossing her arms over it. As he stepped away, he saw the stone break in two.

Chapter 18

ON JUNE 30TH 1908, IN a remote woodland of Siberia, the morning sky was clear and the day was warm. A lone hunter listened for the sound of caribou. Suddenly the sky filled with blue fire so bright that it burned his eyes, even though he shut them tightly. This light was the last thing that the hunter ever saw, and it was the same for the caribou that was less than one hundred meters away.

Those villagers of Kezhemskoe who were awake saw the blue light, too. Those who were still sleeping were soon awakened by the sensation of a harsh force shoving them. The windows of the houses shattered, and a sound like artillery fire could be heard. Believing that the world was ending, the people who had not been knocked down by the blast dropped to their knees and prayed. The world was not, in fact, ending, but an impact had occurred of such magnitude that it could be felt all over Europe.

In the area of impact were to diamonds at the bottom of a crater, one perfect and one so rough that it could barely be called a diamond at all. They were surrounded by miles of felled, fire-lit trees and burning animal carcsses.

If any villagers had dared to venture into the burning woods, they might have found the diamonds and would have become rich. As it was, the two diamonds lay undisturbed for two weeks, four days and nine hours. Then the rough diamond slowly began to expand and take the form of a large, naked black man. He stood up and surveyed the devastation. The man bent over, picked up the perfect diamond from the ashes and climbed out of the crater.

Jude then attempted to convert the ashes into diamond armor, but nothing happened. He knew that his powers were gone and was surprised by how little he cared. What mattered was that he had both arms again. He did not know where he was or in what time period. All he was certain of was that he needed to find some clothes.

Epilogue

In the observation room of the destroyed penthouse, a panicked dog ran circles around the six people lying unconscious on the floor. Tiny, Alma's abandoned Cocker Spaniel, licked Gerron's hand. He stirred, opening his eyes drowsily. The other five woke slowly from their comatose states.

"Dario, are you ok?" Gerron asked.

"Yeah. Was the arctic wasteland we were just in real?" he asked.

Dario turned to see his older brother, Jean-Luc, his body guard, Anatoly and both female scientists, Megan and Sara-Evelyn, get up from the floor.

"Is *this* real?" Sara-Evelyn asked, looking around with wide eyes at the rubble that was left of the apartment and at the smoke filled sky. "Where's the roof?"

They all walked with trepidation over to what had been an outer wall, which was now just a sheer drop of fifty-two stories. They saw the death and ruin in the streets below, and heard the sirens and screams of the survivors. "Terrorists?" Sara-Evelyn asked, almost hopefully.

"You know as well as I do that Alma did this," Gerron responded. "And she's the one who sent us to that hellhole."

"I'm going to try something," Jean-Luc said. He closed his

eyes and took a deep breath. The outlines of his body began to blur and flicker. He stretched longer and shorter, seeming to snap into different shapes before settling into the form of an immense lion. Shocked, Jean-Luc lost his focus and turned back into his overweight self. "So—," he began to say.

"So the powers we gained in that place *are* real," Anatoly finished.

Sara-Evelyn turned to Megan contemptuously. "Too bad *you're* the only one of us who didn't get a special power," she laughed.

"Yeah, too bad," agreed Megan, the wicked smile in her eyes imperceptible to her distracted companions.

Dario climbed without fear to the top of a remaining outer wall, and he rubbed his hands together greedily as he surveyed what was left of midtown Manhattan. "This is going to be a very different world now," he said from his perch on top of the devastation. His palms glowed red as he pulled them apart. "Very different indeed."

Gerron silently watched as his twin made this vast proclamation. He knew that what his brother said was true. He decided to allow Dario his moment of revelry as he gazed at the shadow that Dario's body cast upon the floor of the debris-strewn apartment. As Gerron focused on the shadow of his brother, it rose from the ground and looked with eyeless sight at its master. Wordlessly, Gerron let the shadow Dario know that he was not yet needed, and to lie back down. It obeyed.

Dario was none the wiser on his perch atop the ruined wall. "Gerron," he said, "I want to rule the world."

Coming Soon

MISHA: Resilience

Misha Anime
Concept Artwork
Illustrated by Mikka Manalo

Tennessee A.K.A. Helaxtic

Tennessee Nunez, also known as Tenny, was the first to enter the astral plane of the desert where he acquired the ability to transform inanimate matter into living beings using his imagination. He is the half brother of Jude.

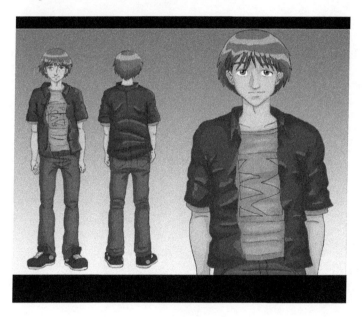

Jude A.K.A. Telaxtic

Jude Dante, a street-tough individual who acquired the ability to transform any matter into diamonds which he can then telekinetically control. His ruthless nature makes him a powerful combatant.

Quintin A.K.A. Cronos

Quintin Koo, a brilliant math geek who acquired the ability to manipulate matter into any size, shape and density he wills making it possible to create new types of elements. Quintin is Tennessee's best friend.

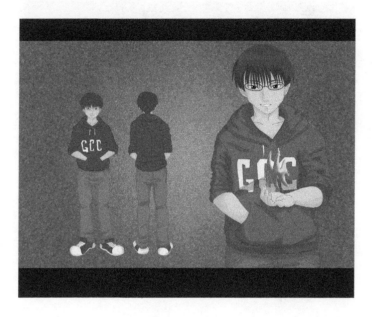

Angelis A.K.A. Sing

Angelis Palle, a beautiful college student who acquired the ability to manipulate the colors of all matter and light. She fell for Tenny after discovering his long-time crush on her.

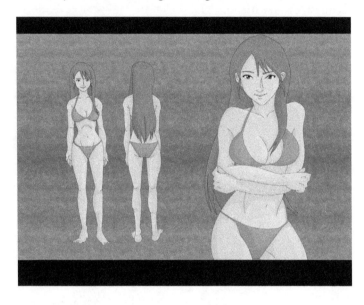

Michael A.K.A. Misha

Michael Soris, a frail young Russian boy with an ability to bestow others with mental abilities. Misha can read minds, but cannot speak directly to anyone as it causes people to fall into a comatose state. Misha was given his abilities by an entity from a different dimension.

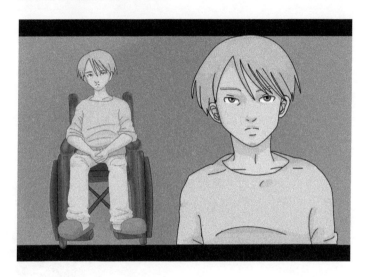

Alma/Corazon

Alma is a little girl who shares her body with an entity known as Corazon. They jointly have the ability to see from a vast distance, the lives of others, and to mimic their mental abilities. Corazon was created by the same entity that gave Misha his abilities.

Frank Lee

Frank Lee is a dangerous assassin. He has no supernatural abilities but is an expert in weapons, hand to hand combat, and stealth techniques.

Lilly Roonka

Lilly Roonka was created by Tennessee as a companion for Angelis. She became the self-appointed guardian and protector of the island.

A Scene from Misha The Island – First Flight

Illustration of when Tenny, Quintin and
Angelis first learn how to fly.

Mishathedesert@yahoo.com